Unspoken

Voices

By

Titilope Sule

Unspoken Voices

Copyright © 2017 by Titilope Sule

Sule, Titilope

Unspoken Voices – 1st edition

ISBN: 9781521744376

Printed in the United States of America

"There is no easy walk to freedom anywhere, and many of us will have to pass through the valley of the shadow of death again and again before we reach the mountaintop of our desires"

- *Nelson Mandela*

To my Family.

You inspire me daily

Table of Contents

CHAPTER ONE - CHANCES ARE

The announcement on the radio gave me a sign of relief "Ghana Airways, now boarding at Gate E". I quickly stood up and got in line. I have to leave, I have no other escape. The police right now are probably on their way to my house. My only hope for survival is that this plane lands in Accra before the police discover that I have fled. As I settle down inside the plane, my mind reflects on the last one year of my life that got me here.

Part One - No Regrets

It is unusual for a guy like me to read entertainment magazines but I became an avid reader ever since I got interested in the lady that worked at Encolag, I bought the Encolag magazine weekly just to read her column. Well, she never gave me any attention despite my multiple attempts to let her know I was a fan of her work but eventually, I got addicted to the magazine.

I remembered picking up the magazine on a Saturday morning and saw the big announcement on the front page. Bisi Adelaja was getting married to Olamide Kuku. Those two were the big power houses being joined together, as in, the Adelajas' owned half of this town and the Kukus' pretty much owned the other half. I sat and daydreamed of how much money I could make in a wedding like this. But this was a restricted deal or so I thought.

Well, before I get into my story, here is a little bit about me. My name is Emeka Obi and I was born 32 years ago as the first child to well-educated parents, owners of an animal farm that was doing sufficiently well to send my three siblings and I through private primary and secondary schools. My father ran the business and my mother stayed home to care for her 4 children. Unfortunately, in my second year in university, I got the bad news that a flood had practically wiped out our town. My parents and siblings were fortunate enough to leave our town but they lost everything they had and were not able to recover much after that. They have only been able to support my siblings to complete their education in public primary and secondary schools.

My siblings and mother hawked groundnut on the road while my father repaired slippers in a little shop he acquired. I, on the other hand, hustled my way through completing my university degree and NYSC, thanks to the generosity of friends and some other runs.

Post NYSC, I left my family behind in Owerri and moved to Lagos to seek greener pastures. I left with only 50,000 naira in my pocket and a suitcase with four shirts and one suit. My father managed to pay my fare with some money he had saved. My entire family was there to bid me farewell. I hugged my father, kissed my mother on the cheek, hugged my siblings and boarded the bus with hopes to make it in big Lagos.

On arriving Lagos, I squatted with an old friend from university and spent two months job searching but yielding no results. I was down to 2000 naira in my pocket and was considering going back to Owerri when I met Chris.

I was introduced to Chris by my host who told me that if I had a strong mind, Chris could help me out. I said I could do anything to make it here. Desperation had set in. This was my last chance.

Chris looked rich. Whatever he was doing was working for him and I wanted to have his lifestyle.

I found out Chris was a high level operation thief. He worked with some clients who had the power to get him and his people invited to high-end social events where he stole money quietly without the knowledge of the celebrants. He also had a group of boys working for him that helped him stage the distraction for key people involved in the celebration. He would then split the money with the clients and paid off his boys from his share. Rumor was that at one birthday party, he was able to walk away with 1 million naira without a glitch in the process.

To be honest, I did not think too much about it. I wanted in. There was no job for me in the market. My CVs never made it into the hands of the hiring managers and when it did, they wanted to know what I could do for them in return for getting the job.

I started off as one of Chris' boys and seven months later, I became Chris's partner. I was sleek, I was fast and I made Chris real good money – I even beat his record. I was finally good at something and it was paying off.

As bad as a career as this was, I was able to send my siblings money for school and built my parents a new home. I also built two new homes in Lagos and rented them out. I had women all over me, they wanted to marry me. I hung out at the best spots in town as a VIP because I spent so much money on drinks that the owners knew who I was. I got invited to the best social events in town (even without my clients' help). I had absolutely no regrets.

Part Two - The Arrangement

In the evening, we met at Madam Okon's spot, our usual hangout location on the mainland in Lagos. The boys and I were busy enjoying our cold beers under the shade when Chris walked in grinning from ear to ear. He had a paper with him which I recognized as the Encolag magazine I had just read. He walked up to me giving me our usual handshake.

Chris: Oh boy, how far nau?

Me: I just dey my guy. Abeg grab a seat and join us. Drinks on me today.

Chris: Ooooh, my guy!!! You are making my day get even better. We got to talk oh, business don land.

Another guy in our group, Bayo, joined in.

Bayo: You know we are always ready to hear wetin dey. Oya spill it. My body don dey hot, you know how money dey always shack my body.

Chris: Bayoooo, your body too dey hot. Anyway, this is the deal. You remember Chief Sanjo? The oga that hooked us up the deal in Warri?

Bayo, so anxious to hear the new deal nods his head quickly and signals Chris to get to the deal quickly.

Chris: Well, he came to my house this morning to show me these papers.

13

Chris hands out a copy of the Encolag magazine and it is passed around but there seems to be confusion on everyone's face.

Me: So what's the deal with the paper? Is the magazine company having a party or what?

Chris: My Guy, you've got to think bigger. See the wedding on the front page? That is the deal!

Me (laughing): Dude you must be crazy. Do you know who these people are?

Chris: Of course I do. I thought it was crazy too but Chief Sango has a wonderful plan to get us in. Look guys, we have an opportunity here to make the biggest amount of money than anything we have ever seen in our lives. Emeka, with the money we can make here, you can start your own business and get a life for yourself. I already have my plans oh, I already started making plans for the shopping center that I want to open with this money.

I had heard the same speech from Chris multiple times before.

Me: Dude, I know what this deal is but this is crazy! We could get in to big trouble for this. These guys are probably getting the biggest security that will pick up on our plans in a minute.

Bayo: You too dey think too much. Abeg Chris, go on.

Chris: I said don't worry. Anyway, I have worked things out with Chief Sango on the details. He could only get the three of us in so it will be Emeka, Bayo and I. Don't worry guys, I will settle the rest of you something from the deal.

Chris laid out the plan for how to get the money out and move it. As usual, one of us had to get friendly with the bridesmaids in charge of the money. To avoid security from suspecting anything, we would have to monitor who got the money out of the hall and into the car and seduce the person until we could get to where the money was. I was picked to be the seducer. The other guys would monitor me and make sure that the other bridesmaids are distracted as well.

To fit in, we had to rent expensive cars and we had to look rich. Chris ordered clothes for us to wear and paid all the expenses for us to look the part. We were all set.

Part Three - The Encounter

I was at the gym working out on my favorite treadmill when I spotted her. I guess she was new to the gym because I never noticed her there before. She came in with a friend and they both headed straight into the locker room. She must have been gone for 15 minutes because I counted through every second of the next four songs waiting for them to come out so I could start a conversation with her. She eventually came out and went to the elliptical machine.

I stayed on my treadmill for another 10 minutes trying to figure out the best way to approach her without getting the killer eyes that ladies usually give when their friends are around them but nothing came up in my head. So I decided to just walk up to her.

Me: Hey, good morning.

To my surprise, she smiled and said good morning.

Me: I don't mean to interrupt you but I noticed you were new here so I wanted to say hello and if you need help with anything, let me know. My name is Emeka by the way.

I really did not know when I became the gym assistant but it was the only thing that made sense to say at that time. She stopped moving and stretched out her hand for a handshake.

Funmi (laughing): Hi, I'm Funmi. I'm actually not new here but I've been gone for about five month. So thanks for offering your help. That was very kind of you.

I was flattered, she was feeling me and I noticed her friend's gaze, staring intently at us so I had to go in for the kill quickly before Funmi noticed.

Me: Sorry to interrupt you guys. Would you like to have lunch with me sometime? Maybe tomorrow?

Funmi: Hmm...tomorrow is booked, I have to help my sister out. How about next Saturday? I will try to make some time for you.

Me: You promise?

Funmi: Yup. I promise.

So we exchanged numbers and I left the gym grinning. Once, I stepped outside I did my happy Igbo dance. I turned around and realized she had seen me through the gym windows and was laughing. I smiled back shamefully, got into my car and left.

Saturday came around and I was so excited. I had been anticipating this day the entire week and actually visited the gym everyday hoping to see her but she was not there so each time, I left disappointed. We spoke the day after we left the gym and planned for 3PM lunch.

I got there a few minutes late, thanks to the unpredictable traffic in Lagos and she was already there having a drink. I walked in and as soon as she spotted me, she smiled again.

Me: Hey Funmi, I'm so sorry to have kept you waiting. I got caught in traffic.

Funmi: That is fine. I know how traffic is in Lagos. Well, we are here so let us not worry about what is out there.

I was mesmerized. Here was someone that I met that I did not have to spend a ton of money on gifts for her before she accepted going out on a date with me. The other girls always wanted something. She was super nice too.

Me: Wow, you amaze me. You don't even know me and yet you are so nice to me.

Funmi (laughing): I don't have a reason to be rude to you either. You are nice too because you offered to help me at the gym even when you did not know me.

The waitress stopped by and took our orders.

Me: So tell me a little bit about yourself.

Funmi: Why don't you start?

Me: Oh, is that how it is? Alright, no problem.

I told her of my background in Enugu and my journey to Lagos but skipped the story of Chris and instead told her I had taken a loan to start a home rental and had grown it into a successful real estate business. She seemed impressed.

Funmi: That is wonderful. There is not much to

know about me. I left Nigeria for college in the UK to study medicine. After college, I returned back and I now work with UNICEF to help treat children so I'm pretty much all over the place. I have no life but it is a very rewarding job.

The rest of the lunch went wonderful; we laughed and made jokes. She had a great sense of humor and seemed to enjoy me teasing her. We ended up staying through lunch and dinner until her phone rang and she had to leave to attend to her sister. We bid farewell and I promised to see her soon. I hoped to see her this coming weekend after the deal was done.

Part Four - The D-Day

The morning of the wedding, we gathered at Chris's place. He had the cars ready. Since I was the main guy, I got to drive a Mercedes Benz G55-AMG. Bayo and Chris rode there together in a Hummer H2. We suited up, stunning in our Ray

Ban sunglasses, shoes by Berluti. Chris went all out for this event.

We skipped the church ceremony and got to the reception an hour late to draw some attention to ourselves. Even before we got in, I caught some ladies staring at us through my sunglasses and gave them a smile but my mind was all on business. The maid of honor was the target and the money was the prize. We found our reserved seats, and started enjoying the night.

The crowd was large, lots of money pushers and celebrities. The food was great, drinks served like no tomorrow. Although we sat in the back, we made sure we could see what was going on up front.

I was on my third drink when I spotted her. At first I thought it was a girl that looked like her but upon second glance, I was almost sure it was Funmi. She was escorting an older guy out of the reception hall and my mind went to Aristo chicks that sleep with older men for money but I could not believe Funmi would do that. There was no indication she was the type. I could not hold back, I wanted to make sure I was not being fooled so I tapped Chris.

Me: Hey Chris, I gotta go to the men's.

Chris: Sure, there is still time.

Me: Be right back in five.

I stepped outside the reception hall and walked around for a minute and then I finally spotted her. When she saw me, she looked surprised and walked over.

Funmi: Hey You! What a surprise. What are you doing here?

Me (laughing): I came for the wedding. I'm not stalking you, I promise.

Funmi: You sure? I made the invite list and I don't remember seeing your name on there.

Me: Well, I'm sure you didn't because you did not

know me then, but hey, so you are cool with the bride and groom?

Funmi: Yup. This wedding is the reason I have been running up and down. I'm so glad it is going well and almost over so I can have some breathing space. The bride is my sister and I'm her maid of honor so we have been....

I stopped listening. I went blank with my brain thinking "This is messed up...this is messed up...this is messed up". I was brought back to reality by Funmi shaking my hand.

Funmi: Are you alright? You look lost.

Me: I'm doing good, my head hurts a little bit though, all the noise, you know.

Funmi: Oh, so sorry. I've got some Panadol, maid of honor duties (she chuckles), you want one?

Me: I'm ok, don't worry about it. I'm sure once I stay out for a little bit, it will go away.

Funmi: Eyah, I wish I could help but duty calls.

The bridezilla is probably wondering where I am.
I hope you hang around for a little while, I want
to see those dancing moves you talked about.

Me: Sure, don't try me. I'm a dance floor king.

Funmi: All talk, let us see you in action.

Me: Cool, I will be around.

No, I had no plans of being around. As soon as
she disappeared into the reception hall, I took off
on my heels. I caught an Okada home since I left
the car keys behind on the table. I knew Chris
would kill me if he found out what I just did but I
could not go forward with our plans. Not to her. I
was feeling strange for her, feelings that I never
felt for any woman in my life. No way.

My phone started blowing up 10 minutes later.
Chris was calling non-stop. I refused to pick it up.
I started to feel anxious, I knew he'd be coming
over soon. Many calls later, I switched it off. I got
home, sat on my couch and was lost in thought

for almost two hours when my door was busted open. Chris and Bayo fumed in.

Bayo: So na here you dey? Why you no pick up your phone na? Abi you wan mess up this deal? wetin be your problem?

Chris: Bayo, chill out. Can you stay outside, let me talk to Emeka for a minute?

Bayo, still fuming, steps out.

Chris: Dude, what is the problem? Why did you leave the spot without telling me? Wetin do you?

Me (shaking my head): I can't. This one is different. Those are not the kind of people that deserve this. I can't do it.

Chris's face turns red as he realizes I am about to screw up his deal.

Chris (yelling angrily): What kind of people deserve this? You know dem? These same people that deprive us from living a good life! These same people spend our millions of naira in one day for a stupid party! Na dem kill my mama for street. They leave am there make she die! These same people, now tell me, why don't they deserve this? I am only doing my fair share of what I deserve in life and if you are going to sit there, fine! I am going back to that hall and don't expect me to give you a kobo of what I get from that deal. You hear me? By the way, make you find my 200,000 naira for all the things wey I don pay for. I go collect am tomorrow, shey you don hear?

He paused for a minute roaming around my living room with one hand on his head, fuming so hard but I could not say anything. And then I heard the car zoom off. I had never seen Chris so upset but I expected it. I just blew off at least 2 million naira deal because of a girl. What was wrong with me?

Two hours later my phone buzzed, I thought it was Chris so I ignored it but after a few more buzzes, I decided to look at the screen and realized it was Funmi. She had sent me a text wondering where I was. So I dialed her.

Funmi: Hey, I've been looking for you. I'm outside right now, everyone is dancing, where are you?

Me: I'm so sorry Funmi, remember the headache? Well it did not get any better so I had to leave. I am sad though, I was looking forward to talking and dancing with you.

I could sense the sadness in her voice.

Funmi: That's, ok. Another time, I guess. I hope you get some good rest.

Me: I will try to, so how is the party going? Taking care of the bride?

Funmi: Oh gosh, I can't wait. A few more hours and I will be free.

She was cut short by what I thought was a gunshot.

Funmi: Oh my God, Oh my God.

I called her name several times and waited a few minutes on the phone very worried before she finally answered. She sounded frantic.

Funmi: Oh my God.

Me: Funmi!!! What is going on?

Funmi: Someone just fired a gun. I have to go check on my sister.

The phone went dead silent. I called both Chris and Bayo but they did not pick up their phone. I felt sick to my stomach.

Part Five – Beginning of the End

I was shaken after I picked up the newspaper the following morning. The title read loud and clear "Gunmen Attack Wedding of the Century." I opened the newspaper in fear and read through the details. Two unknown men had opened fire at the parking lot of the wedding and fled away with almost 3 million naira at the wedding. No one was killed but one of the bridesmaids, Funke Kuku, was seriously injured. The description of the gunmen resembled Chris and Bayo. I sunk in my chair. I was not informed there would be guns involved. Immediately, I texted Funmi to make sure her family was ok. A few minutes later, she called me.

Her voice was still shaken.

Me: Hey Funmi, I am so sorry, I just read the news.

Funmi: I know, thanks for checking on us.

Me: Are you doing ok?

Funmi: Not really. I'm actually in my room because we have been advised not to talk to anyone but I can't stand it. The police are all over here asking questions. That could have been me! The bridesmaid shot is recovering, thank God. At least, the only somewhat good news is that I heard the police have a good lead on the men.

Fear gripped me.

Me: Oh, they do?

Funmi: I don't know. I'm just worried. What if they had killed someone? My sister is so shaken. She cannot even go on her honeymoon because she has to stay around until the situation gets better. I hope they catch those bastards soon.

Me: I hope they do, too. I gotta go, just wanted to check on you, dear.

Funmi: Thanks. I will call or text you later.

I changed my clothes and burst out of the house. I arrived at Chris's house and he was in there with Bayo and the guys. They were celebrating their success. I stormed in and grabbed Chris by his collar.

Me: What the hell were you thinking man?

The other guys quickly jump in to save Chris. I got shoved into the corner. Chris straightened

31

his shirt and walked up to me. He looked like a lion ready to pounce on its prey.

Chris: Are you mad? You have the nerve to show up here? Where is my money?

Me: I will give you your damn money when you tell me why the hell you had to fire gunshots at the wedding? Do you know one of the bridesmaid was injured? Funke Kuku of all people. Do you know what you may have gotten us into?

Bayo jumps into the conversation.

Bayo: She was not co-operating and security was coming near so I had to quicken the situation so we could get out of there. Ol boy calm down. Nothing dey.

Me: Oh really? I have information that the police is on your tail right now.

Chris (waving his hand): Did you come here to scare us? Abeg comot from here. Just make sure you bring my money by Friday latest else, you may end up like the bridesmaid.

I got up and tossed the 200,000 naira at him.

Me: I'm out. No deals, don't come to my house, if you see me on the street, you don't know me. Just count me out. I'm done.

Bayo stood there laughing.

Bayo: Ol boy, when hunger chop you for there, you go come back dey beg us. No be so we pick you up from the streets. You come dey do shakara for us. You think those people care about people like us? Wetin they worry you sef?

I ignored him and walked away. Frankly, I was surprised that no one attempted to stop me. Not even Chris. I stepped out and got into my car. As I was about to make a turn into the intersecting road, I heard the police sirens. From my rear view mirror, I saw 2 police cars and some policemen jump out and rush into Chris's house.

This was my cue. I knew that once Chris got arrested, he would implicate me. I had to run for my dear life.

I zoomed all the way home, pulled out the drawers and as they crashed on the floor, I emptied their contents and packed up my bags and headed to the airport, my heart racing. The closest place to flee to was Accra, Ghana. I got to the airport and lucky enough, there was a flight for Ghana leaving in 30 minutes. I quickly bought the ticket, checked in and settled into the plane.

As the door of the plane closed, my mind went to Funmi. She did not deserve this. She did not deserve the disappointment she would get if I ever got caught. I texted her and said, "I have to travel for urgent business, it may take a few months but I promise I will be back. Looking forward to seeing your lovely face again, dear". I did not receive a response from her.

The plane taxied on the runway, started to speed

up, and eventually took off. I breathed a sigh of relief and started to nod off.

I was well into my sleep when we landed in Accra, Ghana. As the airplane door opened, a police officer stepped into the plane with a picture. I knew he was coming for me. My heart was beating faster and harder, I thought it would beat out of my chest. He had handcuffs and two other men behind him. Soon enough, he recognized me, walked up to me and said, "Mr. Emeka Obi, you are under arrest for the theft of 3 million naira from the wedding of Bisi Adelaja and Olamide Kuku, and attempted murder of Miss Funke Kuku. You have the right to remain silent. Anything you do or say now can be used against you in the court of law." My mouth went dry.

I was taken off the plane and placed on the next flight to Lagos, Nigeria in handcuffs with 2 police escorts.

CHAPTER TWO - FLEE

Part One - Love at First Sight

For the third time, Bola came home late at night, drunk and beat me up. I woke up this morning swollen with aching eyes. I had been limping all morning because my tummy hurt terribly. It had received a blow the night before.

My phone rings and it is Nneka, my best friend.

Nneka: Hey girl, what's up?

Me: I am doing ok.

Nneka: Just calling to make sure we are still on for the movies today.

Me: I don't think I can make it, sorry.

Nneka: Nooo, what happened? I was really looking forward to our outing...oh wait, did that bastard touch you again?

I paused for a little bit, wondering if I should tell

Nneka the details of last night. I choose not to.

Me: Let us discuss it later. He is at home, sleeping.

Nneka: Oh my God. Bisi, do you want me to stop by?

Me: No, please don't. I will be fine. Let us meet up next weekend instead, we can see the movie then. I am so sorry.

Nneka: Just let me know please if you need anything, ok?

Me: Thanks hon. I'm ok.

I fake a laugh but I don't think Nneka bought it.

Nneka: Ok hon, see you next week then but I am telling you now, if I do not see you next weekend, I am coming to your house with the police and a frying pan to knock some sense into that husband of yours.

I laugh again. Nneka has always been a no-nonsense type of chick. We met a while back in secondary school and have been best friends ever since. She is currently engaged and planning her wedding while I on the other hand have been married for just over two years. Two very long and painful years.

My name is Bisi and I am married to a monster called Bola. Prior to marriage, I always fascinated about how wonderful married life would be. My parents have been married for over 30 years and are still in love with each other. I always dreamed that my prince charming would find me and we would live happily ever after just like my parents.

I met Bola about 4 years ago on a plane flight from Abuja to Lagos. I was on duty as an air hostess. He was quite an attractive man and I could not resist taking several peeks at him from the corner of my eye as I attended to the business class clients. He was well dressed in a sleek grey suit. I later realized that I was not the only one checking him out when another air hostess pulled me aside mid-flight to have a private discussion.

Air Hostess: Did you notice that guy up front?

I pretended as if I did not know who she was referring to. Then she pointed at him and I nodded.

Me: Yes, I did. What a fine man.

Air Hostess: I noticed he was not wearing a ring and I need you to do me a favor. Do you mind switching places?

Me: Uhmm...

Before I could respond, the bell rang and it was the fine man asking for attention. The other air hostess quickly went over to attend to him. I turned my back to them and then she returned shortly after.

Air Hostess (rolling her eyes at me): He wants you.

With glee, I hurried over.

Me: Yes, sir, how can I be of help?

Bayo (leaning to the side and resting his elbow on the arm rest): Can I get another bottle of water please and your number?

Me: Yes and no, sir.

I turned and walked away and as I did, the corner of my mouth turned upwards in a smile and my heart beat a little faster.

I returned with the bottle of water to serve him and expected him to continue the conversation but nothing happened.

Five minutes later, he pushed the button again. I walked over and this time, he passed me a note asking me for my number. I again responded with a no. He continued pushing the help button every ten minutes to the annoyance of the other passengers. I eventually gave in and told him I will give him my number after we landed. After debarking the plane, he waited at the terminal for and I wrote my number on a piece of paper and handed it to him. A few days later we were out on our first date.

While we were dating, Bola was quite the extraordinaire boyfriend. He would take me on vacation trips to many places - Dubai, Jamaica, America, you name it. I was the envy of my friends and coworkers. My parents loved him as well. Coming from a middle income family, my parents were excited that my suitor was such a wealthy man. With our humble beginnings, my parents contact with the wealthy was usually in service to them. Whenever Bola visited our home, my mother would usually bring out her best cooking and hosting skills and my father would give up his favorite chair for him. Bola of course, was a gentleman, respectful of my parents and always bringing gifts whenever he visited. I also met Bola's family. His mom was very loving welcoming me with open arms however his dad was a bit skeptical about our relationships, however, my charming personality won them over so they approved of our relationship and also the marriage once we got engaged.

Part Two - The Grandiose Wedding

After about a year of dating, Bola invited me to fly to Dubai with him under the disguise of a business trip. While we were out there, he asked for my hand in marriage in a very romantic setting. Bola reserved a private yacht for us that took us out to the sea. We sipped wine in each other's arms and enjoyed the view as the wind blew in my hair and the occasional spray of water kept us cool. We headed back to the hotel for dinner after our yacht ride and as I entered the lobby, there were flower petals left in an undisturbed pathway leading to the restaurant. As we meandered into the restaurant, dozens of flower bouquets were covered in fairy lights, as well as little notes placed in them. I picked each one and read them and they were messages from Bola stating why he loved me. After I read the notes, I turned around to find Bola on one knee, beaming, asking me to marry him. He put the ring on my finger and as he stood to hug me a jazz band emerged to serenade us.

I immediately called my parents screaming at the top of my lungs and in tears. I could not believe this was happening to me. Being the only child to my parents, they were very ecstatic when I informed them of the engagement. My mother finally had the opportunity to show off to all her friends, the grand wedding her daughter would be having. The wedding date was set in six months. It was going to be a big day for all of us.

After the engagement excitement died down, I had time to think about marriage. Was I really ready for the responsibilities of being a wife?

Was I ready to start having babies? Was I ready to live with one man through thick and thin? I had no doubt in my mind, I was.

There was only one problem. I was not too confident that Bola was the man for me. Although he treated me very well with gifts and trips, we had only been together for a short period of time and within that time, I had seen his bad temper and the way he treated his employees. One day, he slapped his secretary in my presence for missing a file after one of his meetings. When I asked him about it, he said "It is just business. I'm the boss and she should not make stupid mistakes like that. We nearly lost that client."

After pondering on the marriage topic for a few weeks, I decided to discuss my worries with my mom.

Me: Mommy, can I talk to you about something?

Mommy: My dear, what is it?

Me: It is about Bola.

Mommy: Is he ok? Did anything happen to him?

Me: No, he is fine Mommy. It is about the wedding.

Mommy: Ah, thank God. So what is the problem?

Me: I am worried Mommy. Bola has a really bad temper. I have seen how people act when he is around. I know he treats us nice but I am afraid that he treats these people badly and could treat me that way one day.

Mommy: Haba, my dear daughter. Bola does not look like that kind of person. He loves you so much. He would never do that to you. I know you love him too so I know you will both have a wonderful wedding and marriage together. Speaking of the wedding, the lace samples for the wedding arrived today, let us pick one now. You know we only have a short time to plan the wedding so we need to make the decision quick.

I agreed and put my worries aside. We were so wrapped up in planning that we had no time to really talk about anything else. The days were going by so fast and there were so many arrangements to be made. The wedding venues had been booked. Bola's family paid for the majority of the expenses. I flew to America, London, and Dubai to shop for my wedding gown and accessories. Nneka was with me all along helping me make decisions. She had better fashion sense than I did so she knew what would fit me perfectly.

My fears cropped up again 2 weeks before the wedding date. Bola and I decided to take a trip to get away from the wedding stress and go on a relaxing weekend getaway. We flew to Abuja for the date and planned to stay overnight and come back to Lagos the next day.

Bola had planned a nice dinner outing for the both of us. At the restaurant while we were eating, a lady walked in. A few minutes later, I caught Bola's eyes staring at her. I tapped him and he apologized when he knew I had caught him. A few minutes later, Bola excused himself and was gone for a while. I also noticed the lady was no longer in the restaurant so I went around looking for him. I caught Bola exchanging numbers with this lady at the parking lot. By the time I walked to them, the lady had left. When we arrived back at the hotel, we got into an argument over the lady. Bola got so furious and slapped me. We did not talk for the rest of the trip.

A day after we got back to Lagos, I got a bouquet of roses delivered at home with the note "I am so sorry babe." Nneka was with me when it arrived and of course, she was curious to know what he was sorry for. I told her.

Nneka: He did what?

Me: Don't tell anyone please, it is kind of

embarrassing.

Nneka: Of course, I won't but have you told anyone else?

Me: No, the only other person I can tell is Mommy but she would probably brush it aside as nothing. She is wrapped up in wedding planning.

Nneka: I think you should still let her know. I know the wedding is coming up so soon but you need to address this with him and let him know it is not acceptable.

I wanted to overlook it so badly. Everyone was excited and I did not want to ruin this happy moment with my worries.

Me: I'm sure he won't do it again. Don't worry about it. He said he is sorry.

Nneka: Girl, are you sure? I've heard these stories before. The guy always say he is sorry then he does it again and again and keeps apologizing. You may want to check that.

Me (laughing): I will do that, oh.

Nneka: Please do.

I never checked it. Bola came by in the evening and it was back to normal. I was too engrossed in the wedding plans to pay attention to what really mattered. Family and friends had flown into Lagos from all over. So much fun laughs with external family members that I did not want to spoil our joyous moment by bringing up the issue again with Bola.

The wedding day came and it was wonderful. I looked so beautiful in my wedding dress. The strapless ivory dress of lace fabric hugged my hips, and flared out a bit in to a short lace-embroidered train. My mom cried so many times. Bola looked very handsome, clean shaven and in a perfectly fitted tuxedo. The wedding was attended by many celebrities and notable people of society. His parents gifted us with a brand new home and 2 new Mercedes Benz, one for him and one for me. I was on top of the world.

After the wedding, Bola and I moved in together. Prior to the wedding, Bola had requested I take some leave from my job to get settled into marriage and I agreed. I requested one month of leave from my job. Bola resumed work a week after the wedding. After three weeks of staying home, I started getting bored so I discussed resuming my old job with Bola.

Me: Hey hon, so I've been thinking.

He grabbed me by my waist and kissed my forehead.

Bola: Thinking about what babe?

Me: I miss flying. I miss my old job, I want to go back.

Bola's face changed into a tightened look and his hands left my waist.

Bola: No, you don't need to go back. I like having you here when I get back from work. Who is

51

going to cook my meals?

Me: I'm sure we can work something out. I can work on flights from 9AM to 5PM. I just need to talk to my boss. I'm sure he would understand.

Bola: I will think about it.

My boss was happy with the schedule and to have me back. MayaFly Airline had just expanded operations into Enugu so they needed all the help they could get. After much persuasion, Bola finally agreed to let me fly again. I was so happy.

However, something changed. Bola would call my phone every hour. He would call the home phone by 5PM and if I did not pick up, he would call me nonstop until I did. I started noticing his time back home was not regular. Some days he would be back at 6PM and other days, he would be back at 10PM. On those days, I would be so worried that I would not sleep until he got back.

After our first wedding anniversary, the

frequency of his absence increased. Whenever I asked him about it, he would say it was work but I noticed his the stench of alcohol on his breath. For the sake of peace in the home, I would ignore it and go to bed.

Part Three - The Second Fight

The second time Bola hit me was exactly a year and three months into our wedding. He came in late the night before and slept in late that morning. I had to leave to go to work so I was out of the house at 8am. I made his breakfast and left it on the dining table.

I later realized that my phone did not charge the night before and I had one cell of battery life left so I switched it off to save the battery to speak to Bola later. The day was so busy; I was on multiple flights between Lagos and Abuja. I called Bola several times during the day but he did not respond. The last flight was scheduled to leave at 3:30pm. My battery was now below ten percent charged so I tried Bola's phone again. This time he picked up. I told him we will be arriving on schedule. He informed me that he did not go to work because he was not feeling good. I assured him I would be there on time to make some tea and take care of him.

We boarded the passengers but as we were about to taxi, the pilot noticed an engine check light came on so he notified the cabin that there would be some delay. My battery was dead when I tried to reach Bola again. I used the pilot's phone to call him but he did not pick up. This delay lasted 2 hours so we did not take off until 5:30pm. With the flight delay and Lagos traffic, I did not get home until 8pm.

I quickly rushed in to the house and Bola was sitting at the dining table. I moved closer to hug him but Bola grabbed me by the neck and pushed me to the wall.

Bola (barking): Where the hell are you coming from?

Choking, I grabbed his hands in attempt to rip them off my throat. I tapped his arms in a panicked frenzy and he released me and pushed me to the floor.

Bola: Now you can talk, where are you coming from?

Me (coughing and gasping for air): I am coming from work Bola. Why are you doing this?

It was only a second, but in that second I saw Bola's hand rise and fall against my face. I gasped in utter shock and raised my hand to touch my burning cheek as the sound of the slap echoed in the silence.

Bola: You liar. Your flight does not stay this late so you better speak the truth.

Me (my eyes welling up with tears): I am not lying! I tried to call you but you did not pick up.

Bola kicked me on to the floor and I screamed in pain, hugging my stomach and rolling away from him in agony.

Bola: Liar! What phone call? I did not get any phone call from you.

Me (getting on my knees and pleading): Because my phone died, I used the pilot's phone number to call you.

Bola: I knew it. So, now you are sleeping with the pilot? You left me at home to go sleep with the pilot!

I looked up at Bola and all I could see in his eyes was rage. He wasn't listening and I felt scared and confused.

Me: Bola, what are you talking about?

Bola continued to beat me. A mess of hands slapping my head and body interchanged with kicks in the stomach, leg, and back fell upon me. I screamed and tears flooded down my face and with each blow I let out a cry, unable to take my breath, unable to move and unable to escape. I felt pain everywhere and all I could do is scream. He kicked me in the stomach and I screamed and curled up to protect myself. He punched me in the face and I cried and held it in anguish. I knew he had been drinking. He was no longer in control of himself. He kicked me. He slapped me. Again and again until he got tired and got up and went to bed. I lay on the floor coughing up blood, bruised and aching all over, for the next couple of hours until I woke up and went to the bathroom to clean myself up.

I couldn't recognize myself in the mirror. There was blood trickling down face from my hair. My left eye was already turning a dark shade of blue and purple and was swollen twice its normal size. I got in the shower and as the hot water hit my battered and bruised body, it turned red in the drain.

The following day, Bola left for work. I showed up to work with my large sunglasses on my nose and before I could even sit down, my boss was questioning me because my husband had called and informed them that it was my desire to no longer work there. I was furious. I left the office and went over to my parents.

My father was very upset and called a family meeting between my family and Bola's family. Bola continued to state to my parents that I was cheating and claimed that we had a fight, not that he beat me. His parents were embarrassed. They chastised him for not being the family man they brought him up to be. Bola apologized for the behavior and begged for my forgiveness. I was advised by my parents to forgive and forget and return to my matrimonial home.

Part Four - The Third Fight

After our second fight, life returned back to

normal. I was no longer working so I was home at all times to cater to Bola's needs. I decided to do what was needed to keep my home. Nneka recently got engaged to her boyfriend so I was also spending time with her to help plan her nuptials. Nneka had grown to despise Bola because of his behavior towards me. She only came around when he was not in and left before he came back. She reminded me many times that I had lost myself in this marriage and my bubbly personality was almost gone. I knew she was telling the truth but I felt helpless. I wanted my marriage to work so I made the compromises as needed.

The third fight happened after our second year of marriage. It was a Saturday and I was hoping to spend some time with Bola but he mentioned he had some business deal to take care of. Bola left our home at 10am and did not say when he would be back. After waiting a while for him, I decided to go get my hair done and have lunch at my favorite restaurant. I finished doing my hair and walked into the restaurant.

There sitting in the restaurant was Bola with the lady we had a fight about in Abuja. Bola was having lunch with her. I felt my heart sink and a pit in my stomach formed. I was so furious. I had been doing everything I could to keep my home together and here was Bola lying to me about doing business and was cheating on me. I walked over to their table and approached Bola.

Me: You are an animal and will rot in hell.

Bola (raising his hand as if innocent): Please please, what are you talking about?

Me: I thought you were doing a business deal?

Bola: This is business. I think you've met this lady before, we are talking about a business deal.

The lady interrupts him.

Lady: What business? And why is your sister insulting you?

60

Me (shocked): Who is his sister?

Lady (looking confused): You? Aren't you his sister?

Me: Oh my God, Bola! Me? Your sister?

I turn to the lady on the table.

Me: Is that what he told you? I am his wife!

Lady: Oh my Goodness! This fool has been telling me he wants to marry me!

Bola: Ladies, please get it together. You are embarrassing me.

Lady: Embarrassing? I will show you embarrassing!

The lady gets up, takes the jug of water and pours it all over Bola.

Lady: Lose my number, I never want to see you or hear your voice again! Sorry madam, I did not know this fool was married.

She left the restaurant and I left Bola there.

Later that evening, Bola returned home drunk as usual and started beating me for embarrassing him in public.

Part Five - Flee

After speaking to Nneka, I went over to the mirror. I could not recognize myself anymore. I was now a shadow of my former self. My face was battered. My eye was swollen and bruised. My lip was thick and puffy. And I was sore everywhere. I finally came to the realization that if I did not act, this would continue to happen to me. It finally dawned on me that this marriage was all about Bola. I gave him whatever he wanted, I cooked whatever he wanted to eat, I slept with him whenever he wanted, and we only went to places that he wanted to go. I wondered how this would end up. I would either end up dead or be too scared to do anything. I was too scared already.

Bola laid in bed snoring loud, deep in sleep. I brought out my boxes and started folding my clothes into them. I had packed three boxes and loaded them in my car and was packing the fourth when Bola woke up.

Bola: What are you doing?

Me: Leaving

Bola (looking surprised): Why babe?

Me: Because I don't want to end up dead.

Bola: C'mon babe, stop playing.

He got out of bed and realized half of the closet was empty. He walks out of the room and comes back in.

Bola: Are you serious?

I ignore him and continue packing up my things. Bola moves closer.

Bola: Babe, if it is because of last night, I am so

sorry. You know I didn't mean to touch you. I was drunk. I had no idea what I was doing.

I was not interested in having a conversation with him so I continued to ignore him. Bola grabbed my hand with force.

Bola: You are not leaving.

Me: Bola please get your hand off me.

I tried to pull my hand away but Bola gripped me tighter.

Bola: And what if I don't?

Unknown to Bola, I remembered what Nneka had said before I started packing and had a frying pan behind me in the closet. Luckily, my second hand was free.

Me: For your own sake, you should.

Bola kept his hold on so I quickly grabbed the frying pan with my other hand and slammed it hard on his head. Bola screamed, letting go of my hand to grab his head. I continued to hit him with the frying pan all over his body. After five minutes of constant beating, I quickly ran out of the door and locked him in the bedroom. I jumped into the car and drove off.

A few minutes later, I knocked on Nneka's door.

Nneka: Girl, what are you doing here? Oh my goodness! Look at your face. Come inside quick, you need to clean up!

Me: I have some stuff in the car if you can help me. Let me get them out before Bola gets here.

I walk over to the car and Nneka's mouth drops open. She hugs me as tears drop down my eyes.

Me: I had to. I could not do it anymore. I can't live with him.

Nneka: You did the right thing, my dear. I'm sure he will come begging but you have to be strong.

Me: Well, you will have to host me for a few weeks until I find my feet. I'm definitely not going back to that house.

Nneka: Girl, anytime. This marriage thing scares me, oh. Your experience was wonderful before marriage, look at you now.

Me: Don't worry, if Peter screws up, I will be there with my frying pan as well.

We both laughed as we lift my bags into her home. The following day, I went over to my parents' house and informed them about everything that happened. My father vowed to never let me go back to the house again and my mother cried as she took me into her arms. I heard Bola showed up there soon after I left to beg my parents for forgiveness but my father chased him out with a cutlass.

About two weeks later, Bola showed up at Nneka's place to look for me. Nneka was the one that answered the door.

Nneka: Yes, what do you want?

Bola: Please I am looking for my wife.

Nneka (shouting): Your wife? So you have a wife? Well she does not want to see you. You better leave before I call the police on you.

Bola: Nneka, please. Help me talk to her. I need to see her.

Nneka: So you can kill her?

I just got back from the salon and saw Nneka shouting at him. As Bola saw me, he walked towards me. I stood still with my defense ready to attack him if he tried to force me to do anything. Nneka also rushed out and grabbed a stick.

Nneka: If you do anything to her, I am going to use this stick on you. You better believe that.

Bola ignored Nneka and turned to me.

Bola: Bisi, I know I have offended you. Please forgive me. I promise to never hurt you again.

Me: You said that many times, it is too late now. I need you to leave right now.

Bola: Bisi, for the good times. Please do not allow the devil to end what we have.

Me: For the good times? What good times? Our marriage has been hell. You left me all the time. You always had a problem with me leaving the house. Is that why you married me? So you can have someone to control and punch on your bad days? So tell me, what good times are you talking about? Please leave right now!!!

I left Bola looking stunned and walked into to Nneka's house. The next day I filed for divorce.

CHAPTER THREE - THE PARK TREE

Part One - Old Warning

Early morning, the guys (Emeka, Tunji, and Eromosele) are having their daily meeting with Oga on the balcony of Oga's house. This is a normal routine for the guys as their day begins at 6:00AM with the same old warning from Oga.

Oga: Abeg, make una no jam my motto for road oh. If I see one scratch, na your monthly salary I go use repair am until I finish to pay mechanic.

Tunji: Oga, you for leave this kind story every day, you know say I don dey drive your motto long time and I never jam person.

Eromosele: Abeg Tunji, na only you never jam person? Me as I tanda so, nobody in the whole of this Port Harcourt fit drive pass me. When I enter road like this ehn...

Oga interrupts Eromosele.

Oga: Abeg make una shut up for there, I no wan hear story. Make una take am jeje for road. Especially you Eromosele wey your eye go dey shine like say na torchlight. As nepa no come give us light, na your eye I dey take see for hia. Where Emeka dey sef? I never hear him voice this morning.

Tunji laughing, shakes Emeka.

Tunji: Emeka dey stand, dey sleep. Oh boy, you sure say you fit handle this kain job so. Na only one week and you resembu persin we dem don beat inside prison.

Emeka (yawning): What is your business? Abi I no dey here so?

Oga: I don finish morning meeting, make una carry una wahala go.

A few minutes later, the guys head out the gate to pick up their taxis parked outside, but are startled by Oga's voice from the balcony above them.

Oga (pulling his ear): I don tell unaaaa oh, I no wan hear story. No come back come tell me say police seize my motto or hia say you enter fight for park and dem fine you.

The guys all respond in unison, "Yes, sir"

Oga: Ok oh, make God bless una go come.

Part Two - The Discovery

The men arrive at the park and are ready to start filling up their taxis with passengers eager to beat the rush hour traffic to get to their job.

Emeka (waving a face towel): Rumuokoro! Rumuokoro! Madam, you dey go Rumuokoro? Come enter hia Madam. Madam abeg nau.

Emeka is not fruitful in convincing the lady to enter his car. He looks over his shoulder and sees Tunji and Eromosele sitting under the tree eating akara and bread. He walks over there to join

71

them.

Emeka: I am so tired of this bullshit. After six years in university and no job, na so my life go be? I don tire oh.

Eromosele: Oh boi, na so we see am oh. Na so we dey manage. You wan chop akara?

Emeka: No be akara dey do me, I never even carry one passenger and Akungba, that tout don collect 200 naira from my hand. Na fuel money be dat. Wetin I go tell Oga when I reach house so?

Tunji: Shebi Oga na your uncle? He go forgive you. Just rob onions for your eye before you go meet am. He go forgive you. Oga no wicked.

Emeka begins to sniff his nose like a stench caught his nose.

Emeka: Eromosele, wetin dey worry you sef? Why you no come baff before you leave house? See as your body dey smell.

Eromosele, angry, and caught off guard by

Emeka's accusations, responded angrily.

Eromosele: You dey craze? No be as you come hia so wey this place start to dey smell. I just talk inside my head say make I no complain. Tunji, you don mess for hia so? This kind smell fit kill persin oh.

Tunji: E gba mi! Ki lon she awon omo kekere yi. (What is wrong with these kids?) Na me una dey take play so?

The guys start to hunt around the area to see where the stench is coming from. Emeka's leg bumps into an object and he tries to kick it away but it is too heavy. As he bends over to the object to lift it, the stench becomes stronger. He notices a nylon wrap around the object, turns it around, then realizes it is a human body. Holding his hand to his head, Emeka screams.

Emeka: Ewoooooooooooooooooooooo!!!

The guys gather around Emeka to see why he is

screaming.

Eromosele: Na wetin be dat?

Emeka: Dem don kill person for this park oh.
Make we go call police.

Tunji smacks Emeka in the head.

Tunji: You dey craze? Which kind university you
go sef wey no give you sense? You want make
police come arrest us say we don kill person.
Abeg make we comot from hia before people see
us oh.

It was too late. Emeka's scream had alerted other
taxi drivers in the park. People gathered around
and begun to lament over the dead body.

"Chei! Na who do this kain thing? God go punish
am oooohh, chei."

"Blood of Jesus. Na all these rich men wey don
use person for ritual, chei see as poor man dey
suffer."

A lady starts to wail, "This na persin pikin oh, na

who wicked like this? Make una confess oh."

Meanwhile Akungba, the local tout had gone to alert the police opposite the park to report the situation. He returns with the police and the crowd begins to dissipate. No one wants to be held accountable for a dead person.

Policeman: Where the dead body dey?

Akungba (pointing to the nylon): E dey dia.

Policeman (walking towards the nylon): Na who find this deadbody for hia?

Everybody keeps quiet and more people leave the crowd. Emeka stares at Tunji unsure of what to do. Eromosele, frightened and shaking, speaks up.

Eromosele: Oga police, nobody kill person for hia oh. Na so we come hia this morning, we come dey smell rotten egg. We come begin dey look for wetin dey smell, na so Emeka come kick the body. Na so we come find am.

Policeman: Na who be Emeka?

Eromosele points Emeka out in the crowd.

Policeman: Oya, make una two follow me come to police station. You must write statement for this dead body.

Eromosele looks confused.

Eromosele: Oga police, no be us do am nau. We just discover the body, how we go take write statement?

The policeman drags Eromosele by the waist and Emeka follows willingly. Tunji hides behind the crowd. As Eromosele is being dragged away and pushed into the police van, he starts to scream.

Eromosele: Tunji!!! Abeg go tell Oga wetin happen, we no kill person oh. Abeg, I no fit sleep for cell.

Part Three - Investigation

The police van arrives at the Police Station. The guys are dragged down from the police van and taken in to write a statement.

Policeman: Come write ya statement. After ya statement is written. You go wait for cell until your Oga come bail una.

Emeka: Oga Police. We didn't do anything. Why do we have to stay in your cell?

Policeman: You dey craze? Na who come kill person for dia? You go stay dia until our oga talk to your oga. If you like, make noise. Na here you go sleep.

Eromosele: Oga abeg no vex. Emeka no get sense at all. We go write statement.

In the meantime, Tunji arrives at Oga's house to report the morning situation to Oga. As Tunji runs into the compound, he meets Oga at the doorstep heading out.

Tunji: Oga oh, dem don arrest Eromosele and

Emeka oh.

Oga: What??? Na wetin dem do?

Tunji: Oga, na dead body oh. Emeka find dead body na so police carry dem go?

Oga: Jesus Christ! Which kain wahala be this so? This one no be small wahala oh. Why dem no leave the dead body alone. Driver!!!!!!!! Tunji, Abeg go call my driver for me make we go dia now now. You know the police station dem go?

Tunji: Yes sir, I know where dem carry dem go.

Oga and Tunji arrive at the police station.

Oga: Good afternoon, I have been told that two of my boys are in your cell.

Policeman: Good afternoon. What are their names?

Oga: Eromosele and Emeka.

Policeman checks his book registry.

Policeman: Yes. I see their names. They have

been jailed while we investigate the murder of the dead body.

Oga: Why will you jail them? They did not commit any crime.

Policeman: Oga, you can't talk that oh. So who killed the woman? Your boys were found at the scene of the accident.

Oga: Abeg make I see your oga, your DPO. I'm not ready for your nonsense talk.

Policeman: Oga never come work. You go wait for am.

Policeman points at the wood bench in the corner. As Oga sits down, he sees the sign "Police is your Friend" and shakes his head.

Later that afternoon, DPO walks into police station and walks past Oga into his office. Oga was sleeping so he missed the DPO entrance. Tunji taps Oga to wake him.

Tunji: Oga wake up oh, e be like say DPO don

enter.

Oga (yawning): Oh, he don enter office?

Tunji: Yes, sir.

Oga walks up to the policeman.

Oga: I hear that your DPO is around. Can I see him?

Policeman: Oga no be like that nau, you go first settle me before you see my oga. The ink wey your boys take write statement no be free. Na 2000 naira you go pay.

Oga: Look my friend, I don't have time for your rubbish. See how you wasted my time waiting for your DPO? I will make sure you are sacked if you don't allow me see the DPO right now.

Policeman suspecting Oga may know one of his superiors, changes his tone.

Policeman: Oga nau, na play play I dey do you so. See as you come dey vex for me. We dey try for here, abeg na, put something for pocket.

Oga gives policeman 500 naira and policeman walks him to DPO office.

Policeman (in salutation): Oga, sir, these are the people waiting for you, sir.

DPO: Please come in and have a seat. It is my understanding that you want to see me.

Oga: Yes, sir. Two of my boys are in your jail cell as we speak for reporting a dead body found in their park this morning.

DPO (looking at the policeman): What is the situation here?

Policeman: Oga DPO, we go arrest dem. Dem no wan confess who kill the person. We still dey investigate.

DPO: Sir, that is the situation. Until we find the murderers, we cannot release your boys because they may run away.

Oga (interrupts): But these guys are not guilty. Is it a crime to report an incident in this country?

DPO: Oga, you have to understand. We have seen many cases where these criminals run away after being bailed.

Oga: So what is the next step?

DPO: I will give you a call, give the police man your number. Here is my card. I am sure we can handle the matter. Be expecting my call.

Back in the cell, the guys sit each with their heads in their hands. What have they gotten themselves into, one of the boys thought.

Later that evening, Oga receives a call from the DPO.

DPO: Ha, Oga, how is everything?

Oga: Apart from the fact that you have refused to release my boys, all is well.

DPO (laughing): Oga, we have to do our duties, you should understand. I want to come and see you at home. Is it ok for me to come now?

Oga: I am expecting some visitors in the next two

hours so if you come quick, it is fine. I live on number 23 Akpan Street. If you reach Okporo Junction, just follow the road facing the MTN store until you reach the mango tree. Turn right at the mango tree, you will see one woman selling groundnuts in the corner. When you see the woman, Akpan Street is opposite her. My house is the first white house on the left on that street.

DPO: Ok, I am on my way. Arrange 100,000 naira ready if you want to see your boys tomorrow.

Oga: DPO, that is too much nau. Abeg reduce the money nau.

DPO: Oya get ready 80,000 naira. Just for you.

The DPO arrives thirty minutes later and money is exchanged. The following morning, Oga arrives at the police station and Emeka and Eromosele are released.

Three weeks later, the police arrested Akungba

at the park. A witness had tipped the police that Akungba, the tout, was seen stabbing someone in the dark the night before the body was discovered.

?

CHAPTER FOUR - LOVE LOST

Part One – Separated

I sat in class during my break studying hard to understand the problem my teacher just gave to us. My name is Ejiro Anaborhi. I grew up in Benin City, Nigeria but my parents both hail from Delta state.

My parents got married 25 years ago. I heard they tried to have many children before me but each time, my mother would either have a miscarriage or a stillborn child. This issue created strife between my parents and eventually their families. Rumors spread across my village that my mother was incapable of carrying a child. For a woman in our town, this was a terrible stigma. Since they lived in the rural area of Delta, they did not have sufficient funds to travel to the city to seek better health care. In spite of their differences, my parents stayed together until my mother got pregnant for the ninth time.

Once my mother realized she was pregnant, she separated from my father because she feared losing her baby. Perhaps my father's family had curses that prevented her from bearing her children. My mother moved in with my grandmother until she gave birth to me. She never returned to my father's house and the marriage was dissolved shortly after that.

After I turned six years old, my mother remarried a different man and took me back to my father's home to live with him as her new husband did not want to raise another man's child. My father, never remarried and not knowing how to take care of me, called on his sister, Aunty Tega, to take me with her to Benin, where she lived with her three children.

Aunty Tega, who seemed warm and friendly when she visited my dad to pick me up, became quite monstrous once we settled in her home. My Aunty Tega would buy new clothes for her children but selected used clothing for me from our local market. Aunty Tega never let me eat on the table with her children. I ate in the kitchen only after I was done doing the dishes. Aunty Tega sent her children to good schools in our community while I was told to sell oranges at the local market. Aunty Tega often reminded me that neither of my parents wanted me so I dared not attempt to run away. She was my only hope. She also told me that she did not have money to send me to school because my parents never sent her money.

The other women in the market where I sold oranges thought I had no parents because they never saw anyone with me.

Aunty Tega had evil ways of showing discipline. One day, I had returned from the market to meet Aunty Tega in the living room.

Me: Aunty, Good Evening.

Aunty Tega rolled her eyes at me.

Aunty Tega: Where is my money? How many oranges do you have left?

Me: I sold 5 for 250 naira but one man took my orange in the market and said he will give me the money tomorrow.

Aunty Tega: What did you say? You give my orange away for credit?

She walked towards the kitchen, picked up my plate, and dumped my food in the trash.

Me: Aunty, please. I am very hungry, I never chop today.

I felt hungry all day, so much that now it had turned into pain.

Aunty Tega: If you don't shut up now, you will end up outside!

Me (crying): Aunty, please. I beg you in the name of God. My belle is paining me.

Aunty Tega refused to give me any food. I sat in the kitchen crying. I drank some water and soon slept off. The following day, I went back to the market and the man owing me the 50 naira for the orange was not at the market. When I got back home, Aunty Tega kicked me out of her house and told me not to return until I came back with her money.

Part Two – Lost and Found

When Aunty Tega kicked me out of her house, I had no way to reach my parents. The only other place I knew was the market so I went back there and slept there overnight on the floor, cold and hungry.

The following morning, when the market women arrived, I walked around and begged for food and money. Since they knew who I was, they were very generous to me. I found one shack where disabled people stayed and I slept there with them. This became my routine.

My shoes became worn-out so I walked around barefooted. I could not afford a haircut so my hair grew and eventually became a rough dada (dreadlocks) style. I became familiar with everyone and after sleeping in the market for a week, one of the market women offered to have me sleep at her home until my parents came looking for me.

Surprisingly, after about four months, Aunty Tega showed up at the market looking for me to take me back home. I returned back to her house but nothing changed. I still sold food at the market and cleaned up the house afterwards. I still could not attend school. Sometimes, people would visit our house and Aunty would hide me in the room and command me not to come outside.

One day I overheard her discussion with a visitor from my hiding place.

Aunty Tega: Welcome oh, how are my people in the village?

Visitor: They are doing fine. Where are the kids?

Aunty: They have gone to school, but they will be back for Holiday during Christmas.

Visitor: That is good. You are very strong for taking care of these children since their father died.

Aunty Tega's husband had passed away a few years earlier.

Aunty Tega: It is God's mercies.

Visitor: What of Ejiro? How is his school?

Aunty Tega: We are managing but that boy is always giving me problem. He won't listen to his teachers at school. I don't know what to do anymore.

Visitor: God bless you oh. You know Mama Ejiro will be very happy with how you are taking care of this boy.

The mention of my mother jolted me up. Since I lived with Aunty Tega, I never heard about my mother. I did not know if she was alive or not and I was too scared to ask Aunty Tega. I opened the door and stepped outside. The visitor's mouth dropped open.

Visitor: Jesus! Who is this?

Aunty Tega: Ejiro!!! What happened to you? Why are you looking so dirty? I told you to stop playing dirty in school.

I stood still shaking.

Me: Aunty, I go to market not school.

Visitor: Is this Ejiro?

Me: Yes ma, do you know my mama or papa?

The visitor drew me closer to her and started wiping the dust off my clothes.

Visitor: Yes, I do. How are you? How is school?

Me: I am not in school. I sell oranges at the market, I just got back.

Visitor: What? Aunty Tega, is that true? After all the money Papa Ejiro sends to you?

There was no response from Aunty Tega. Instead she stared angrily at me.

Visitor: Ejiro, take this 1000 naira ehn. I have to go now but I will come back and visit you.

I held on to her clothes, crying.

Me: Please don't go, I want to see my mommy! Please Aunty, don't go! Take me to my mommy!

The visitor managed to release my grip from her clothes with many promises that she will be back. Aunty Tega stood there fuming and speechless.

When the visitor left, Aunty Tega went outside to get some bamboo sticks. She asked me to lay down on the table with my shirt off. I begged her but without mercy, the bamboo sticks were shattered on me until my skin bled. I went to bed that night with no food.

Part Three - Reunion

I was selling oranges in the market when a strange lady approached me. She had a warm smile and as soon as she saw me tears welled up in her eyes. She bought some oranges from me and asked me for my name. After buying the oranges, she walked over to another stall to buy some other items. I could not stop staring at her. I noticed she talked to the stall owner and kept staring at me. After about 20 minutes, she walked over to me again.

Strange Woman: Ejiro, where is your mother?

Me (surprised): I don't know where she is. How do you know my name?

She smiled.

Strange Woman: I knew you when you were very little. Where is your Aunty Tega?

I became scared and she noticed.

Strange Woman: Don't worry Ejiro, I won't hurt you. I am looking for your Aunty Tega. Do you know where she is?

I nodded my head. She bent over in the middle of the market, hugged me and picked me up. I began to cry. After a few seconds, she put me down.

Strange Woman: Ejiro, I am your mother.

My eyes widened and I jumped on her.

Mother: I am so sorry Ejiro. I tried to find you but I did not know where your aunty lived. Your father would not tell me. I am so sorry. I want to take you home.

Me (crying): Please take me! Aunty is very wicked. She beats me too much!

Mother: Oh my God! My poor boy. So this is what will happen. I will go to Aunty Tega's house and I will tell her I want to take you somewhere you can learn how to sew so you can come back and be sewing for her. If she asks you if you want to go, say yes. You hear?

I nodded my head. The strange woman now identified as my mother watched me for an hour before she left. After I was done selling, I left the market and went home. As I entered the living room, I saw Aunty Tega and my mother having a discussion. Aunty Tega called me back to the parlor.

Aunty Tega: Do you know this woman?

I shook my head.

Aunty Tega: Ok, this woman is a friend of mine and she wants to take you somewhere to teach you how to sew. Do you want to go and learn how to sew?

Me: Yes, ma.

Aunty Tega: Ok, when you finish learning how to sew, you will come back to Benin and I will buy a machine so you can be sewing here.

Me: Thank you, Ma.

Aunty Tega turns to address my mother.

Aunty Tega: You can take him. Only for three months, oh. If not, I will tell his father.

Mother: Ah, no worries. His father will not even know I was here.

Aunty Tega: Ok.

I packed up my two torn shirts and left with my mother that night. The following morning, we boarded a bus and headed back to a strange town. On arriving, my mother took me to a house. She told me it was my father's house. A man was sitting outside biting on a chewing stick.

Mother: Papa Ejiro, thank God I met you at home.

My mother pulls me up front.

Mother (fuming): Do you know who this is?

My father looks dazed to see my mother and shook his head.

Mother: You see your son? This is what your wicked sister has done to my son. She turned him into a house boy. After all the suffering I went through to have this boy, you and your sister want to ruin his life? Do you know this boy has never been to school?

Father: What do you mean? This is Ejiro? How did you see him?

Mother: May God punish you! This was the plan between your family ehn? To not allow my son to be something in life! I always knew it! Evil people! Wooooooooooooo! All the wickedness you have done to my son will surely come back to your family!

Father: Please no insults here. What was I supposed to do? It is also your fault. You left the boy with me after you got married to that useless husband of yours. Which kind of mother will leave her only child for somebody else?

Mother: Thank you very much. I have taken my son back. I never want to see you or any of your wicked family around this boy. If you come around him, anything your eyes see, you take.

I stood there quiet watching the exchange and staring at their faces. It was my first time ever seeing them together.

Mother held my hands and walked back to the road to catch a taxi. She took me to my new home with her husband and I met my baby sister. I was enrolled into a school program and was the oldest in my class.

CHAPTER FIVE - VICTIM OF SOCIETY

Part One - Where is my Daddy?

Sade walks into the room with her handbag hanging on her arms and her keys on her hand. She walks around the room and drops her bag on the table. Femi, her son, runs out to hug her.

Femi: Mommy! Mommy! Mommy! Look what I made!

Femi hands her a piece of drawing he made. It was a picture of Sade.

Sade: Aww my prince, this is so sweet. It looks beautiful. Have you done your homework?

Femi: Yes, I have, Mommy.

Sade smiles and hugs Femi again.

Sade: Good boy. For being such a good boy, what do you want Mommy to get for your 10 year old birthday?

Femi looks down looking sad and slowly

mumbles his words.

Femi: I don't want anything, Mommy. I just want to see my, Daddy.

Sade's smile suddenly changed into sadness and she paused for a moment staring into space as she remembers her past.

Part Two: Found the One

Sade is knocking on the door. No one answers the door so Sade picks up her phone to dial her Mom.

Sade: Ekale, Ma (Good Evening Ma). I just got home, I lost my keys and I'm outside, please can you open the door for me?

Couple of minutes later, Mama Sade opens the door and Sade walks in to see her dad sitting in the living room talking on the phone. As she walks in, she greets both parents and is about to walk to her room but is stopped by the call from her dad to return back to the living room. Mama Sade takes a seat next to Baba Sade.

Baba Sade: Wait, wait, come back here. Where are you coming from?

Sade: I went out, dad.

Baba Sade angry with Sade's response fires back.

Baba Sade: Am I stupid? Of course I know you went out. That is the reason I am asking you, where are you coming from?

Sade: I went to a restaurant to eat with a friend.

Mama Sade joins in.

Mama Sade: What kind of food are you eating that you are coming back at this time of the night? Your mates are married with children and you are out eating with friends? I have asked you a million times, when are you bringing your husband to come and meet us? I am already getting old oh, I want to see my grandchildren.

Sade does not respond to her Mom's query. An

awkward moment follows for a few seconds and then her dad follows calmly.

Baba Sade: You know we want the best for you.

Sade: Yes, dad, I know. I was actually on a date.

Mama Sade jumps up in her seat on hearing Sade's response.

Mama Sade: Ehen, now we are talking. Who is he? What does he do? Who are his parents? We don't accept just anybody in this family. When can we meet him? When is he-

Baba Sade yells at Mama Sade to stop harassing Sade.

Baba Sade: E fi omo mi sile. (Leave my child alone).

Sade smiles at her parents

Sade: Very soon, I will bring him to introduce him to both of you.

Mama Sade (grinning so hard and rubbing her

hands together): Ope oh (Thank God). Oya, you can go and sleep. Have you eaten?

Sade laughing.

Sade: Yes ma, I just came back from a restaurant.

Mama Sade: That is true. Good night my dear. We still have to continue our story oh but go and rest first.

Part Three – What is Our Future?

The following evening, Sade and Kunle are strolling together, holding hands and laughing. They find a bench, Sade takes the seat and Kunle follows.

Sade: That show was so funny. Thanks for taking me there, I had so much fun.

Kunle: Yeah me too, thanks for coming out again. You look beautiful by the way.

Sade (blushing): Thanks.

Kunle staring hard at Sade, continues to say.

Kunle: You know, I just noticed your eyes.

Sade: What about my eyes?

Kunle (still staring hard at Sade, goes on to say): They glow when you smile. Like they pop. Really pop. I love them.

Sade grinning from ear to ear looks up to Kunle and Kunle kisses her on her lips softly. Sade then turns away laughing.

Kunle (smiling): What is so funny?

Sade: Nothing, just having fun. How often do you go around giving compliments?

Kunle: I am not that type of guy. Do you see me at parties often? I'm not out there like that. I like to stay anonymous. It takes a special kind of girl to get my attention.

Sade: Uh huh. Well, I better get home soon.

Kunle: Why the hurry?

Sade: You know my parents got on me last night when I got home late. I don't want the same questioning today.

Kunle: But you are a grown woman.

Sade: Yes, I am a grown woman still living with my parents so I have to live by their rules.

Kunle: So why don't you move out?

Sade: I don't see the point of moving yet. I'm not married, and I save a lot of money staying with them. They want to meet you by the way.

Kunle is taken by surprise at Sade's last statement. Sade notices Kunle's reaction.

Sade: What is the problem?

Kunle: No, no problem at all. I was just caught off guard. So when can I see them?

Sade: I can tell them when you are ready. Maybe next week?

Kunle (touching his chin): Hmm..next

week....next week. Oh, that won't work out. I have to go on a business trip.

Sade: What business trip? You did not tell me.

Kunle: Sorry, my boss just informed me today. You know how my job is. I'll be gone for a while, it seems. I think about two months.

Sade's face drops even more. Kunle pulls Sade forward then kisses her on her forehead.

Kunle: I promise to make it up to you.

Sade: I feel so sad and a little disappointed. I was hoping you would be able to see my parents soon. They are really excited to meet you. Can't you stop by before your trip?

Kunle: This week is quite hectic at the office. I have been working late as you know and now I have to prepare for this trip. I promise, I will make it up to you when I get back.

Sade: That's fine. I'll let them know.

Kunle (smiling): That's why I love you. You are

so understanding.

Part Four - Missing

Sade is knocking on her friend's door. Her friend, Ayo, opens the door and Sade runs inside in tears.

Ayo: Haba, Sade. Are you ok?

Sade prances up and down the living room, sobbing uncontrollably.

Sade: Ayo, I'm dead. I'm dead oh.

Ayo: Stop saying that jo. What do you mean by you are dead?

Sade still prancing about the room continues.

Sade: Kunle has killed me Ayo. Kunle ti ba aye mi je (Kunle has ruined my life). I am pregnant and I have not heard from him. He won't answer the number he gave to me before he left. I have been calling and calling since he left and he won't answer.

Ayo places her hand over her mouth with shock on her face.

Ayo: Oh my God. How long has he been gone and when did you find out?

Sade (still in tears): I found out last week but he has been gone for almost a month now. Ayo, what am I going to do? My parents will kill me. How can I tell them? How do I tell them? What do I do?

Ayo: You have to calm down first, Sade. Let us think about this.

Ayo holds Sade's hands and takes her to a seat.

Ayo: So the pregnancy is about a month old and no one has noticed so that's good. We need to think fast. You can't be a single mother. Your parents will be so disappointed.

Before Ayo finishes her statement, Sade's phone rings and she turns off the phone.

Ayo looks curiously.

Ayo: Who is that calling you?

Sade: It is one old man. He came into my office last week and I gave him my business card to follow-up on business and he has been disturbing me since then about going out. Abeg forget him jo, my life is in shambles now.

Ayo: Is he Nigerian?

Sade: Yes. His name is Chief Adeyemo. Why?

Ayo pauses for a few seconds and then hops around excited

Ayo: Hmm I think God is giving you a solution. You have to go out with him.

Sade: No. Did you not hear me? I said I am pregnant for Kunle. How will he solve my problem?

Ayo: Exactly! You can go out with him and let him claim the baby. You know. Either that or you have to abort the child. And I already know abortion is not your solution. This is a better solution.

Sade pauses to think for a few moments and starts to cry again.

Ayo: Stop crying dear. Do you want to end up a single mother? No man will want to marry you with your child. Please think about it. Do you want your child to grow up with a single parent? Please do it for your child's future.

After thinking for a few minutes, Sade dries her tears, picks up her phone and dials Chief Adeyemo.

Sade: Good afternoon Chief....Yes Chief...Friday evening is fine. I will meet you there.

Sade hangs up the phone and looks at her friend.

Ayo gives Sade a comforting hug and Sade leaves.

Part Five - Household of Chief Adeyemo

Iya Kola, the first wife of Chief Adeyemo is sitting in front of her mirror opening her drawers searching. She walks away from her drawers and moves to the bed to look around. Raising the mattress, she starts shouting.

Iya Kola: Hmm, where has my gold bangle disappeared to oh? If I start talking now, it will be as if I am starting trouble. I know I kept it in this drawer. Wunmi! Wunmi!

After a few seconds, Wunmi walks into the room.

Wunmi: Yes, Ma.

Iya Kola: I know you will act as if you did not hear me. Where is my gold bangle?

Wunmi (shrugs): I don't know.

Iya Kola: I kept it in the drawer here and the only women living in this house are you, your mom, and myself so one of you must have taken it.

Wunmi: I did not take anything. Is there

anything else?

Iya Kola (clapping her hands): Yes oh, there is.
Oleeeeeeee!! Oleeeeeeee!! (Thief, Thief) Please
bring out my jewelry for me!

Iya Wunmi, second wife and mother of Wunmi,
walks in.

Iya Wunmi: What is going on here?

Wunmi: Mommy Kola's gold bangle is missing
and she called me in here to accuse me of
stealing it when I know nothing of it.

Iya Wunmi: Ha-ha! Mommy Kola, kilode? Did
you see Wunmi take your bangle?

Iya Kola (hands on the waist): Who else will
wear my bangle if it is not you or your useless
daughter talking to me like I am her mate?

Iya Wunmi (shouting): It is you and your
children that are useless!

Iya Kola: My children are very successful oh,
they are not useless as you already know. Unlike

your children, coming in and out of the house like jobless people.

Chief Adeyemo and Kola, the first child of Chief Adeyemo both walk into the room.

Kola: Mom, you are disturbing the neighbors. I don't want them to call the police again. Please can you keep your voices down?

Iya Kola: No, I won't oh, they have stolen my bangle and if they don't produce it right now, the entire neighborhood will call the police for me.

Kola: What bangle are you talking about, Mom?

Iya Kola: My gold bangle, the one Chief bought for me last month.

Chief Adeyemo: Oh! I saw it in the parlor last week and I kept it for you in my drawer since you were not in. I think you left it in there.

Iya Kola: Are you sure?

Iya Wunmi: You see yourself? You have been exposed. Next time, check well before you call my children into your mess. If not, you will see my trouble.

Chief Adeyemo: I don't know what is wrong with you women, always making noise. This is even a good time to tell you people that I am bringing a new wife in to give me rest. I am tired of all your wahala. I need some peace in this house.

Iya Wunmi, Iya Kola, Kola and Wunmi stare at each other in total shock.

Part Six – Reunion

Eight months later, Kunle is waiting in an office and Kola walks in. Kola talks to the secretariat and takes a seat next to Kunle. After a few stares, he recognizes Kunle.

Kola: Hey, excuse me, are you by any chance Kunle Ajayi?

Kunle: Kola!!! My God! Look at you!

They both stand up to hug each other.

Kola: It has been what? 15 years at the least. Wow! See you oh! You are a grown man, from your orobo days.

Kunle: Abegi, see who is talking. You shortie, you don tall oh. Almost my height now.

They both laugh and hug each other again

Kola: So what have you been up to? How are the folks? So nice to see you again.

Kunle: Mehn, lots lots! Family is good. I just got married you know.

Kola: Wow! Congrats man, congrats! That is a big step!

Kunle: I know man, life just changes. So do you live in this town?

Kola: Yeah I do. I am shocked that we have not crossed paths until now. Abi were you living somewhere else?

Kunle: Nah, I have been living here but I was out of town for a while. I just got back.

Kola: My goodness. Welcome back man. Nothing has changed. You know you should come by the house this evening. My dad will be so excited to see you.

Kunle: For sure. Let me have your address and I will stop by. Even bring my wife with me so she can meet my old family.

Kola: Yes, man, that would be great!

Part Seven - New Replaces Old

Iya Wunmi is in the kitchen cooking and Iya Kola walks in.

Iya Wunmi: Can you imagine how this small girl called Sade has just come in here and taken over our house and husband? Chief does not even pay me any attention anymore.

Iya Kola: Well, such is life. You did the same to someone else. Don't you remember?

Iya Wunmi: Not the same way Mommy Kola did.

This girl is not even as old as my first child. What an insult. Chief is just carrying her everywhere and showing her to his friends. We need to put an end to this.

Iya Kola: So, what can we do? I'm sure when he gets tired of her, he will find someone else. She is just enjoying now because she is still young and carrying his baby.

Iya Wunmi: I won't wait oh. I'm just feeling sorry for her now because she is almost due. Once she has that baby, she needs to join in the housework and we need to do timeshare because he is our husband too, not only hers.

Iya Kola (laughing): E se se bere ni. (You have just started.)

The evening arrives and the Adeyemos are having dinner, chatting and laughing at each other's jokes. Kunle and his wife are present with them, catching up on old times. A few minutes later, Chief Adeyemo and Sade walk in, hand in hand. Sade is gleaming until she looks across the table and freezes.

Kunle, the man she had put in her past for eight months is staring her in the face. Kunle looks stunned to see the woman he abandoned now pregnant and in the hands of his childhood best friend's dad. Chief Adeyemo notices the stares.

Chief Adeyemo: Sade, is everything ok?

Sade: Yes dear, everything is fine. I'm just feeling a little dizzy. Please excuse me.

Sade excuses herself from the dining room and in that period, Chief Adeyemo notices Kunle's presence. He hurries across the room to hug him.

Chief Adeyemo: Haaa! My boy, is this you? God is great. Small boy like you, you are now bigger than me oh. You used to run around with that big tummy, eh? It is all gone now. What do they call it again (rubbing Kunle's stomach)...errrrmmm six pack, your tummy is hard. How is your mom and your little ones?

Kunle (laughing): They are all fine, sir. Meet my wife, sir.

Chief Adeyemo: E gba mi (Help!). O ti oh (No oh), when did you marry? And I was not invited? I don't agree oh, you are not married yet until you have dobale (prostrate) in my presence.

Kunle prostrates for Chief Adeyemo.

Chief Adeyemo: Ehen! Now we are talking. Iyawo mi, how are you dear? Welcome to my home. Anything you want to eat, just name it. This is your home too. Don't be shy. Kunle is my son eh, welcome my dear.

Sade walks back into the room.

Chief Adeyemo: Before I forget too, Kunle, see, I'm trying to keep up with you young boys. Meet my wife, too. Sade is her name, see she is expecting my new baby.

Chief Adeyemo turns to Sade.

Chief Adeyemo: Sade, meet my son, Kunle.

Sade shakes Kunle's hand, slightly bending her knees while managing a smile.

Sade: You are welcome to our home.

Kunle: Nice to meet you, too.

Chief Adeyemo: Oya let us eat, many things to celebrate. I am so happy today to see you, Kunle.

Half way through his meal, Kunle excuses himself to go to the bathroom. A few seconds, Sade mentions she has to go to the kitchen. She finds Kunle on the balcony and approaches him.

While shoving him, she speaks.

Sade: How dare you? Look at what you have done to my life.

Kunle: Sssshhhh, this is not the right place.

Sade: Yes, it is, because I don't know the next time I will see you. Just like you disappeared on your business trip. Look at me. Look what you have done to me.

Sade starts to cry.

Kunle: I'm so sorry. I did not mean to disappear on you. The project got tight and I did not have the time to contact you.

Kunle's wife is searching for Kunle but on hearing the voices of Kunle and Sade, she pauses to listen to the conversation.

Sade: Oh shut up! But you had the time to date around abi? Or are you telling me that girl you came with is not your girlfriend?

Kunle: She is my wife actually, we got...

Sade: My goodness! I am finished. You do this to me and run away? You get me pregnant and go off to marry another woman?

Kunle: What? I thought the baby belonged to Chief Adeyemo!

Sade: No fool, this pregnancy belongs to you.

Kunle's wife walks in on Sade and they both keep quiet immediately.

Kunle's wife: I just can't believe my ears, wow, this is unbelievable.

Sade burst into tears and covers her mouth for the second time as Chief Adeyemo comes into the meeting area.

Chief Adeyemo: What is going on here? You people left us at the table for some time. Your food is getting cold. Haba, Sade why are you crying? Somebody tell me what is happening?

Kunle: I will let Sade tell you herself, sir.

Sade: I'm so sorry, sir. I didn't mean to.

Chief Adeyemo (looking confused): Didn't mean to do what?

Kunle's wife: The baby that she is carrying belongs to Kunle.

Chief Adeyemo in shock starts to laugh. Kola, Iya Kola and Iya Wunmi walk in.

Chief Adeyemo: No, you can't be serious. Shebi we just met Kunle today. How is that possible? Kunle, is that true?

Kunle: I'm sorry, sir, I did not know she was your wife. I just found out today.

Chief Adeyemo: Wait! You just found out she is my wife today or you just found out she is carrying your baby today, which one?

Iya Wunmi and Iya Kola start to make some noise.

Chief Adeyemo: Shut up, you women, or get out.

The wives both keep shut and listen attentively.

Kunle: Both, sir. I just found out both, sir.

Chief Adeyemo closes his eyes. Sade goes on her knees to beg Chief Adeyemo.

Sade: I am so sorry Chief, it was the devil. Kunle got me pregnant and ran away. I did not know what to do.

125

Chief Adeyemo: Aye mi oh. Sade! Do you think I am a fool? As I am looking at you now, before I count to three, I want you to get out of my sight. I don't even want to see you in our bedroom, just pack your load and get out before I land on you!

Sade picks herself up from the floor and runs out of his sight. Chief Adeyemo walks away disappointed as his wives giggle behind his back and celebrate quietly.

Part Eight – Rejected

Kunle knocks on the door of Sade's home and Mama Sade opens the door.

Mama Sade: Yes, can I help you?

Kunle: No ma. I mean, yes ma. I am looking for Sade.

Mama Sade: Is she expecting you?

Kunle: Yes ma.

Mama Sade: Ok, come in and have a seat, let me get her for you.

Mama Sade calls out for Sade to come in and see her visitor.

Sade walks into the room shocked to see Kunle standing by the door.

Sade: What are you doing here? Have you not ruined my life enough? How did you get my address?

Mama Sade: Kilode? Calm down, you know you are having a baby soon.

Sade still hyperventilating and pointing at Kunle.

Sade: Mommy, it is him. He is the one that destroyed my life. The man that got me pregnant and ran away after he said he would marry me.

Mama Sade's face turned angry as she faced Kunle.

Mama Sade: What are you doing here? After you messed up my daughter? Are you here to marry her now? What have you come here for?

Kunle: To apologize ma. I honestly did not know. If I were not married, I would have...

Mama Sade: Oh! So you are even married. Just wait here let me call my husband for you. Baba Sade! Baba Sade oh, come and see the man that ruined your daughter's life. Kunle, just wait here oh, I'm coming. Baba Sade!!!

Before she returns, Kunle leaves the house in fear and Sade continues to sob. Mama Sade returns with soap mixture in a bucket.

Mama Sade: Where is that boy? Where is that foolish boy?

Sade: Mommy, he just left.

Mama Sade: Lucky idiot, God saved him today. What is his name again?

Sade: Kunle.

Mama Sade: Kunle, Ko ni da fun e. May your head be cursed forever, may you never know peace. You will never succeed at work. May you never...

Sade screams as her water breaks.

Part Nine - Back to Reality

Femi shaking Sade's arm speaks.

Femi: Mommy, mommy, why are you crying?

Sade (in tears hugs Femi): I am so sorry baby. Your daddy passed away before you were born.

Femi looks up to his mom and starts crying.

Femi: Mommy, but you said he was working in Nigeria.

Sade (holding his face): I know baby, I am so sorry. You were too young to understand. One day you will, I know you will.

⁇

CHAPTER SIX - A WOMAN'S PLACE

Adanma: Education liberates the mind. However, some people like my father would argue that a woman's education is a waste of money because a woman was created to take care of a man.

Part One – Marriage First

My mother got married to my father in the traditional way without having a say. By the time she was 18, she was given away to him - a pure virgin trained to do the house chores of cooking, cleaning, and washing clothes. That was her pride until she gave birth to me and my twin brother, Uzochukwu.

In her days, the men were trained to be warriors and the women were trained to care for the men. My father, Nnamdi, was the greatest warrior of Umona Village. When it was announced that he was searching for a wife, all the mothers prepped their daughters for the wedding day.

The wedding day came along and the women were paraded in front of my father to make his choice. The girls wore a cloth over their bosoms and around their waist to accentuate their figure. They each served him a meal in which he took a taste as part of the judgment. My mother claims she knew he would pick her. She was one of the finest women in the village of Umona and was a great cook as well. To no surprise, he did. As you see, my father knew no better.

The missionaries had arrived and set up schools in Umona village but my father refused the white man's education. He was too proud to sit in a classroom and have another man tell him what to do. He also refused education to my mother as her duties remained in the kitchen.

When we turned six years old, my mother secretly met with a missionary that offered to come to the house to teach Uzo and I how to read when my father was out farming. My mother would hide the books under our bed and warn us not to tell my father that we were being educated.

We were almost 18 years old when my father finally changed his mind. He came home fuming one day because a stranger had cheated him off the money from his cocoyam sales. That year had been a good harvest year for my father and instead of harvesting cocoyam and giving it to his friend to sell for him, he decided to sell them himself so he would not have to split his profit. Unfortunately for him, on the first market day, after talking to his friend and boasting of his good sales, he realized that the stranger had deceived him. As he walked in, he called our mother.

Papa: Mama Uzo! Mama Uzo!!!

Mama: Yes Papa Uzo, what is the matter?

Papa: Can you believe this? A whole me. Somebody cheat me.

Mama (looking suprised): How do you mean?

Papa: Chai! That man is so lucky oh. If I catch him in this village ehn. Where is Uzo?

Mama: The children are playing in the backyard. Uzo! Adanma! Come and greet your father.

Papa: No, I only need to talk to Uzo.

It was too late. We both came dashing across the compound.

Papa: Uzo, my boy. Do you want to go to school?

Uzo looked confused and looked at my mother. She nodded her head at him. I was very excited that Papa would finally let us start school.

Uzo: Yes, papa, I want to go school.

Papa: Good boy. Tomorrow, you will go to school.

I quickly spoke up.

Adanma: Papa, I want school too. Can I go?

Papa turned to me, bent over and held my face.

Papa: No, Adanma, who will help your mother in the kitchen when you go to school? You have to stay with your mother so you can learn to be a good wife and one day, a good man will come and marry you. If you go to school and don't learn how to cook, no man will marry you. Do you want that?

I shook my head as tears rolled down my face. I was young and naive. I wanted to go to school but I had been raised in a society where marriage brought honor to women.

The following day, Uzo started school. Each day, I would take his notes and he would show me what he learned in class. We would both act the plays out and laugh at ourselves.

Part Two - Choosing my Path

As I got older, I noticed other girls in our community going to school and I approached papa again. This time mama was on my side.

Adanma: Papa, I need to ask you something.

Papa: Yes, my beautiful daughter, what is it?

Adanma: Papa, I want to go to school. Ogechi and Ngozi are now going to school. Why can't I go?

Papa: Because I will not waste my money to send you to school when you will end up in a man's kitchen after you marry.

Mama: Haba papa Adanma, that is not completely true. I have been watching that thing that show people...em, television and they show woman doing good thing. One is president, one is govanor, maybe one day our daughter too can be govanor. My own Adanma, govanor of this state. Don't you like that?

Papa: Those women don't have shame. My own

daughter must get her honor in this village.

Adanma: But papa, those women are respected everywhere they go. They are doing good things for their people.

Papa: What good things? Instead of them to stay home and look after their children, they are going everywhere so who is looking after their children at home? Are those good mothers?

Adanma: But Papa, all my friends are going to school.

Papa: Let them go, you stay at home. By the way, have you given any thoughts to the marriage proposal from Mazi Kenechukwu's son?

Adanma: Papa, I am not ready for marriage.

That sentence must have shocked him because he spat out his tobacco and stared at me like I had spoken a forbidden word.

Papa: Ehn? Did I hear you well?

Mama joined in.

Mama: Yes, papa Adanma, she is not ready to marry. Besides, their son is too old for my daughter. That man is over 40 years old.

Papa: And so? The man is rich. He can take good care of her.

Mama: Money is not everything. You were not very rich and I married you so let my daughter make her own choice.

Papa: The both of you are not serious. Mazi Kenechukwu will be here with his son next tomorrow for formal introduction, you better be ready.

Two days later, Okoronkwo, Mazi Kenechukwu's son arrived with his father for the formal introduction with kolanuts and palm wine. Both families accepted the marriage proposal, the bride price list was provided to the groom's family and a date was set for my igba nkwu.

I sat in my room furious about what had just

occurred. I had no say in my own future. My traditional wedding was in two weeks. As the night came, a thought came into my head but I had to wait until dark to carry out my plan.

In the middle of the night, I crept to the headmistress's house, a missionary called Mrs. Johnson. I knocked quietly for a few minutes before the door was opened.

Adanma: Good evening, Mrs. Johnson.

Mrs. Johnson: Yes, what are you doing out so late?

Adanma: Please, I need to speak to you, can I come in?

Mrs. Johnson: Sure, come on in.

She made tea for me as I admired her neatly kept home with interesting furniture from abroad.

Mrs. Johnson handed me the cup of tea and invited me to have a seat.

Mrs. Johnson: So, what is it that is so urgent that

you would like to speak to me about? Do your parents know you are here?

Adanma: My father wants me to marry. I want to go to school, Mrs. Johnson.

Mrs. Johnson: That is no problem. I can stop by tomorrow to speak to your parents.

Adanma: Oh no, it will be too late. My father will not listen. They have agreed on my bride price, my igban kwu is in 2 weeks. I need help. I want to leave this village.

Mrs. Johnson: I'm sorry, Adanma, I cannot help. That will be a crime on my part. I am so sorry.

Adanma: Please, Mrs. Johnson, I cannot marry. I want education. I want to be governor. I see those women on TV. I want to be like them. I will marry later, I promise. Please, help me.

Mrs. Johnson shook her head and asked for me to return back home.

I returned home disappointed. My hopes of

having an education had been dashed.

My igba nkwu day arrived. I woke up that morning and the house had never felt busier. Family relatives strolled in and out. The women were cooking in our backyard, while the men were setting up the tents. The entire village had been invited as Mazi Kenechukwu was the richest man in our village and Okoronkwo was his first son.

My mom came into my room as I was thinking about what was about to happen.

Mama: My beautiful daughter, how are you doing today?

Adanma (looking down): I'm fine ma.

Mama: What is the matter? Today should be your happiest day, have you looked outside?

Adanma: Yes mama, I have but I don't want to marry.

Mama sighed.

Adanma: I know my dear, but papa has insisted this is what he wants for you.

Adanma: What about what I want. Does it not matter?

Mama: It does, of course but papa is the head of this family and makes the final decision. I am sure he will not do what is wrong for you. Mazi Kenechukwu family is a good one so they will take good care of you. And you know I will always be there for you.

I paused for a minute.

Adanma: I went to see Mrs. Johnson.

Mama: What for?

Adanma: I wanted to run away.

Mama: Ewo! Why, my daughter? Do you want to kill me?

Adanma: No, mama. I just wanted her to help me get into school. I don't want to marry. I feel so sad every day when my friends are telling me about school.

Mama: I understand. Me too, I wanted to go to school but your father won't let me. We don't always get what we want in life but God knows best. Please take your mind off this and be happy ehn. All these people came to see you today. You can worry about school tomorrow, ok? Please smile for me.

I forced a fake smile.

About two hours later, I was being prepared to be presented as a bride. The festivities had started outside. There was a band playing, people were eating and the groom's family had just arrived. The groom, Okoronkwo, looked very happy. He and his family ushered to greet my father and then showed his seat. I peeped through the window in my room, hoping the clock would move very slowly and the hour would never arrive but it did.

I carried the iko filled with palm wine to find my

143

husband. As I walked through the crowd, the men cheered inviting me to bring it to them. My father was seated in front, gleaming with pride. My mother seated next to him was smiling as well. Somewhere in the guest area was Mrs. Johnson. We both locked eyes and she looked at me with pity. I continued and finally found Okoronkwo. I knelt down and gave him the palm wine to drink and the crowd cheered. Three hours later, after much eating and dancing, the wedding was over. I bade farewell to my family and left to be with my husband in our new home.

Part Three - The Breakthrough

One week after our wedding, there was a knock on the window. Okoronkwo was snoring heavily and did not move. I stood up, tied my wrapper and went to the door. There was a note slipped under. It read, "Come and see me tomorrow at midnight - Mrs. Johnson." My heart skipped a beat. I quickly tore the note and went back to bed.

The following night, while Okoronkwo was sleeping, I managed to sneak out of the house. As soon as I was out of the house, I ran to Mrs. Johnson. I only had a few minutes before he would notice I was gone. I knocked on Mrs. Johnson's door and she opened the door quietly and ushered me in. She looked around to make sure no one had seen her pull me in. As I came into her living room, I saw mama.

Adanma: Mama! What are you doing here?

Mama: ssssshhhh!!!

I quickly quieted down and she handed me an envelope, hugged me and started walking away. I held on to her hand.

Adanma: Mama, wait, what is going on?

Mama: That is all I've got. It also has your bride price. Take it and live your life. Go to school. I want you to be happy. Make sure you come back and see me before I die.

She hugged me again and left before I could say a word. I was shocked and speechless.

Mrs. Johnson sat me down.

Mrs. Johnson: Do you really want to go to school?

Me: Yes, but can you tell me what mama was doing here?

Mrs. Johnson: Your mother came to me three nights ago. She told me about her life story and how she never had a choice on her life. You have a choice and she wants you to live your life before it becomes too late. She wants you to do something other than clean after your husband for the rest of his life. She begged me to help you do that. After listening to her, I gave it a thought and I decided to help you but we have to do it quick. We don't have time.

Adanma: What can I do?

Mrs. Johnson: You have to leave Umona tomorrow night. I have arranged for a vehicle to pick you up and take you to the city. My good friend, Anne, will be waiting for your arrival. She will take care of the rest. You will live in the city with her and start your education. She has offered to pay for everything and also help find you a job when you are finished. For now, go back home before your husband finds you missing. Meet me here at midnight tomorrow.

I was ecstatic but also very scared. What if Okoronkwo finds out? What if papa finds out I am missing? That will hurt him.

I quickly hurried home and slipped into bed.

The following day, while Okoronkwo was gone, I packed up a bag and hid it in the living room. In the middle of the night, I picked up the bag, crept out and headed to Mrs. Johnson. She was waiting for me when I arrived. We left her place very quietly with a lantern and met with a strange man. I got into the car, bade Mrs. Johnson farewell, and the car drove off.

Part Four – The Return Home

I left Umona at eighteen years old shortly after my marriage. The drive took me to the car park and I boarded a bus to Lagos to start school. I studied under the supervision of Mrs. Anne and took the university entrance exam and passed it three years later.

It was not so easy to get here as I had thought. Mrs. Anne wasn't quite nice as Mrs. Johnson had described her. Mrs. Anne was divorced with no children and worked at the British Embassy. When I arrived there, there were two other girls living with her. She made us wear uniforms and do housework for her after school.

At Mrs. Anne's house, we had a strict schedule.

We all woke up at 5:00am to do the morning cleaning, and then went to school. After school, we changed back to the house uniforms and made lunch and dinner. Between lunch and dinner, we cleaned up the yard, even though there was no dirt in it. After dinner, we did our homework and cleaned the house again. The routine continued the following morning. Mrs. Anne liked her house sparkly clean. She would scream each time she saw a speck of dust anywhere. She scared me each time she screamed but soon after, I got accustomed to it and learned to ignore it. The other girls had been living with her for a year and told me horrid stories about her. She never let us leave the compound except when we left for school. She was worried the neighbors would call the police if they knew she made us do work. On the outside, she acted like she adopted us. On the inside, she acted like we were her slaves.

Sometimes, I thought about mama and papa back

home and longed to see them. Mrs. Johnson sometimes sent letters from mama and Uzo to me and I would write back to her. I did not hear from papa.

After graduating from the university, Mrs. Anne was kind to find me a job at a bank where I met Charles Orji. He proposed to me five months after I met him and I accepted.

Charles requested to meet my family. Although scary, I knew it was time to return. Mama told me Okoronkwo had remarried two more wives after I left. Also, Papa had broken his arm after he fell from a coconut tree this year. Uzo had also returned back to the village to set up a clinic.

On arriving in Umona eight years later, everything seemed different. I saw signs of schools. The roads were developed, there were more buildings than I ever remembered. I could not recognize the place anymore. My parents still lived in the same house so after questioning a few villagers, we were able to locate the house. Papa was sitting out front on his favorite chair and Mama was selecting Ugwu leaves for dinner. I asked Charles to remain in the car while I approached them first.

Mama was the first to notice me. She threw her tray of ugwu leaves in the air as she ran to hug me. She spun me around many times as if to confirm that I was truly her long gone daughter.

Mama: Adanma, is this you?

Adanma: Yes, mama.

Mama screamed, started rolling on the floor with her hands in the air, thanking God for my return. She got up again, spun me around and got on her knees this time, repeating the same thanks.

My heart felt the pain of leaving them and seeing them this way brought tears to my eyes. It was as if a lifetime had passed. Papa sat in his chair. As I walked closer to him, I noticed he had tears in his eyes. I knelt down next to him and started begging for his forgiveness. He stood up, lifted me up and gave me a hug. Mama joined in the hug and we were all in tears. I noticed Uzo was not around.

Adanma: Mama, where is Uzo?

Mama: He is at the clinic, he will be back soon.

Mama then noticed the car and the young man in the car.

Mama: Who is that?

Adanma: Oh, mama, that is the man that wants to marry me.

Mama jumped up and down. Papa joined in the excitement, walking to the car. Charles stepped out of the car to greet my father.

Papa: Really? You are welcome, my son.

Charles: Thank you, papa.

Mama: So when is the wedding date?

Adanma: Haba! Mama, we will discuss that one tomorrow.

Mama: Are you still not ready to marry?

Adanma (laughing): No mama, I brought him here so of course I am.

Mama pulled in a bench for us to sit and went in to prepare some refreshments.

Both mama and papa were interested in my long journey living by myself and meeting Charles and his family.

As I recounted the tales for them, I realized I took a huge risk but it was a risk worth taking for my life. In the end, I had one life to live and I was glad I made the choice for me. We set the date for my igba nkwu.

The entire village had heard I returned and showed up for the ceremony. The only person missing was Okoronkwo.

CHAPTER SEVEN - THE BOARDING EXPERIENCE

For few, boarding school was fun. For many like myself, boarding school was a haunted place of terror. Looking back now, I laugh at my memorable journey through secondary school. I laugh only because I survived but not everyone did. I knew I always wanted to go Lackett Secondary School since my friend Ahmed said that was his school of choice. Ahmed and I have been best friends since primary school. We lived next to each other and our parents were also good friends. My name is Ali, here is my boarding school story.

Part One - Newbies on the Block

Our parents drove off as Ahmed and I dragged our iron suitcase up the stairs to check into the dorms. We were in our new well ironed uniforms beaming and excited to start this new experience together.

We got through checking in with the housemasters tearing through our boxes, emptying it and looking for contraband items. After checking us in, they gave us our room number. Ahmed and I were roommates as requested by our parents. On arriving in our room, we started to unpack all our items on our bed to be arranged neatly into our closet. I recall Ahmed presented me with a new watch that his dad bought for the two of us as gifts. We were just about done arranging our clothes when Senior Ugonna walked in.

Senior Ugonna: Hey, you two. What are you two doing here?

We stood frozen to the spot. Ahmed managed to muster a response.

Ahmed: We are unpacking our luggage.

Senior Ugonna: I can see that. Are you new to this school?

We both respond in unison nodding our heads.

Senior Ugonna: Ok. In 5 minutes all new students are to assemble in the dining hall for hostel rules. Make sure you are there on time.

As Senior Ugonna walked away, we quickly packed away the rest of our clothes and provisions on our bed back into our box and headed towards the dining hall.

The hostel rule meeting was very brief. There were two senior members that gave rules on our weekly schedule, lights out, sanitation Saturdays. After the hostel rule meeting, we were served dinner and returned back to the hostel.

Upon entering our rooms, we noticed our boxes had been ransacked. We quickly went through our items to make sure everything was secure. I noticed the watch Ahmed gave to me was missing. We stared at each other confused, not knowing who to report to, we informed our housemaster about it but he stared at us foolishly and told us next time to lock our boxes and closet before leaving our rooms. I resigned to my fate that the watch would be gone forever until 3 days later when I saw the exact watch on Senior Ugonna's hand. He was showing it off to his friend.

Ahmed and I ran up to him to confront him. Big mistake.

Me: Senior Ugonna, please can I see your watch?

Looking suspicious, he showed it to us.

Senior Ugonna: Do you like it?

Ahmed: Please, Senior Ugonna, that watch looks the same as the one my father gave Ali. Can you remove it so we can check?

Senior Ugonna getting agitated fires back at us.

Senior Ugonna: Are you crazy? Can your father afford this watch? My father bought me this watch almost two years ago. If you are missing a watch, I am sure it is not this one. Find your watch elsewhere.

Senior Ugonna had such a hostile look on his face that we walked away in fear immediately.

Later that night, after lights out, Ahmed and I were falling asleep when someone opened the door to our room and switched on the lights. It was Senior Ugonna. He asked us to follow him. Like obedient slaves, we walked behind him to his room. He asked us to kneel down and raise both of our hands. He was punishing us for embarrassing him.

Senior Ugonna went to bed and we were in punishment until the following morning. Of course, once we knew he was fast asleep, we took a break with each of us serving as a guard for the other sleeping until the following morning.

Part Two: Massacre

Massacre. A word I never heard until I entered Lackett. My first experience with massacre happened in my second year. We just concluded our final exams and it was nearing the Christmas holiday so the school was having the annual Christmas dinner, serving the special fried rice and one piece of fried chicken. This was one of the rare times we had fried chicken in our menu.

We were all lined up according to our classes, all eager to eat our special meal. I got a peek into the dining hall and noticed the colorful linens that were placed on the table. I also noticed the white covered bowl that contained the rice and chicken. My excitement rose.

Finally, we were all in the dining hall. The prayer was said and we each started to dish our meals.

As I waited for my turn, I heard some noise in the back and people screaming Massacre. I noticed a rush of students jumping over the tables, running all over the room, grabbing people's food and in some cases, the bucket of food. Ahmed stared at me confused.

Ahmed: Ali, what is happening?

Me: I don't know.

Before we could say abracadabra, one of the students had come over our table and in attempt to steal our bowl of food, slipped, and our bowl of food went flying in the air. Ahmed and I jumped trying to catch what was left of the rice and chicken flying all over the place. Ahmed managed to catch a piece of chicken and we shared it laughing so hard at all the madness.

I looked over my shoulder and saw Senior Ugonna hurrying away with a bowl. It was time for revenge. I screamed "Massacre!" and pointed to him. A group of guys saw him and ran over him, grabbing the bowl of rice and again, it went flying high in the air. This time, I ran and grabbed a piece of chicken from his bowl and ran away before he realized who was around him. Senior Ugonna managed to grab one student as he struggled off the floor. I felt pity for the student.

The housemasters did not seem bothered by the chaos in the dining room. They had their special seating and were deep into their rice and chicken, laughing and pointing each time someone got hit or fell. After eating, they eventually got up and put order to the room. At that time, it was too late. There were bowls everywhere, rice and chicken bones all over the dining floor, and some students had begun fighting. The housemasters separated the fighting students and ordered all of us back to the hostel right away. My sympathy was with the cooking women that had taken the effort to cook the meals. They not only wasted their time, but now had to clean the mess the students had created all over the dining hall. Ahmed and I relied on our provisions for dinner, laughing as we recapped the night event especially the scene of Senior Ugonna falling over.

Part Three: Rub and Shine

There was no water running out of the taps that morning. Fortunately, I had a spare bucket of water so Ahmed and I managed the bucket of water by bathing our crucial sanity areas. By evening, there was still no water so Ahmed and I had to join the other boarding students lined up by the water tanker to fetch water to shower the following morning.

As we marched out of the hostel, I heard my name being called. I recognized the voice. It was Senior Ugonna. We pretended to not hear him and walked faster but he continued to call our name. Determined to not respond, we continued walking faster.

Based on my past experience, in a situation like

this, the senior students usually send us junior students to fetch their bath water for them. Sometimes, it got as far as us fetching their girlfriend's bucket of water too. So on the average, the junior student ended up fetching up to four buckets of water. One for him, one for the senior student, and two for the senior student's girlfriend. Being that the junior student hands can only carry two buckets of water that meant getting in line twice, which meant you could waste almost 3 hours of your time fetching water. Senior Ugonna was especially known for sending junior students for fetching 5 buckets of water because he needed two buckets for his size per bath and his girlfriend. That meant almost 5 hours dedicated to his water needs.

I heard footsteps closer to us and soon enough, my head was bumped with a bucket. I turned around and Senior Ugonna was right behind me.

Senior Ugonna: Ali! Didn't you hear me calling

your name?

Me: No, Senior Ugonna. Ahmed did you hear?

Ahmed shook his head profusely.

Senior Ugonna: Take these buckets and bring the water to my room.

Senior Ugonna handed me six buckets.

Me: Senior Ugonna, I have tests tomorrow. I cannot finish fetching all the buckets.

Senior Ugonna: Ok, Ahmed, help your friend.

Ahmed: I have the same tests too.

Senior Ugonna: Not my business, the both of you figure it out.

Senior Ugonna walked away. We did not have any tests the next day but we did not want to dedicate our evening to fetching water either. Lucky for us, we bribed another student with provision to help us so we were done fetching all the buckets in 4 hours including ours.

Exhausted, we kept our buckets of water under our bed and went to bed.

The following morning, we woke up to get ready for school. We pulled out our buckets and it was empty. I froze for a moment and then felt overwhelmed with rage and sorrow. Someone had stolen our water while we slept. We went around the hostel looking for our bucket. We found it in the bathroom empty.

Ahmed and I borrowed a bowl of water each from our classmates, brushed our teeth, washed our face, sprayed cologne all over and went to school.

Part Four - Survival

Ahmed and I had made it through 2 years of boarding school and were still alive. We thought we had been through every punishment and knew every trick in the book. This particular incident proved me wrong.

It was sanitation Saturday. On being admitted to the school, we were each placed in a school hostel building and there were 4 school hostel buildings. Sanitation Saturday was held every two weeks and involved all the school houses competing for cleanliness of their hostel buildings. The housemasters representing each house took this competition seriously because the results were announced to our principal and this was quite shameful to the housemaster if their house came in last. Sanitation Saturday involved cleaning your rooms, the hostel bathrooms, the walkways, and everything else that was within vision. The inspectors, the housemasters and some senior prefects, walked around and rated each hostel's cleanliness.

That morning, Ahmed woke up coughing and sneezing. The medical center was only open to emergencies on weekends so he could not get some medicine. I helped Ahmed clean up our room with the other roommates. Unfortunately, we could not get the window completely done by inspection time. We tried to cover the dirt in Ahmed's window as well as we could.

The inspector's walked in, all looking firm and checking every corner for a chance to give the hostel less score. Ahmed stood in his corner and we were all silently praying that the inspectors would overlook his window. Our prayers were not heard. An inspector walked over and asked Ahmed to move away. Ahmed moved away slowly and the inspector opened the curtain. He gasped as if he had seen a ghost. All the inspectors hurried over and quickly got to their notes scribbling.

When the results were announced at our breakfast, we came in last.

After breakfast, our housemaster called Ahmed over to see him and we did not see him until much later. Ahmed was asked to cut a full lawn of grass with cutlass for making our house come in last place.

By that evening, Ahmed was terribly ill and had bumps on his leg. He could barely speak. I quickly reported his situation and a medical van was called to take him to a hospital.

Ahmed's parents were notified that he was ill at the hospital. They came down to the city on the same day to see their son. Furious at the state they found their son in, they stomped into the principal's office on Monday morning and I was asked to narrate the incident to the principal of the school. The principal apologized for the incident and the housemaster was suspended. Ahmed's parents informed my parents of the situation.

Both Ahmed and I were withdrawn from the school and taken back home to be day students. I was happy to be home again.

CHAPTER EIGHT - SAVE HIM, SAVE ME

My name is Gloria Edidiong. I am 35 years old. I have no children. I used to have one, his name was Akpan Edidiong. This is my story.

Part One – Uncle Johnny

I grew up in a face-me-I-face-you with both of my parents but I never lacked love. My parents did everything within their power to make sure I was well taken care of. My father was a taxi driver and my mother was working in the primary school as a teacher. This was what my Uncle Johnny told me.

When I was 8 years old, my father was killed in a car accident by armed robbers that wanted to steal money from him. My mother died shortly after that from severe hypertension. After my parents' death, my uncles in Calabar took over my care to assist but could only do so much. I was eventually transported to Port Harcourt to live with my Uncle Johnny.

Uncle Johnny was very nice to me and set me up to start my secondary school. Uncle Johnny worked in a shop and would bring back buns for me from work. When he got back home from work, he would read to me and tell me all these wonderful stories about my parents. This continued for so many years and I became so fond of Uncle Johnny. His wife, Aunty Dayo, was not too fond of me. She always complained that Uncle Johnny was spending too much time with me and I should be playing with my mates instead of spending so much time with him. They did not have any children so Uncle Johnny took me as his child. Aunty Dayo eventually stopped complaining and accepted me as her child.

Part Two - The Close Stranger

Aunty Dayo had travelled for her work training for 3 days so it was just UNCLE Johnny and I at home. I had just returned from school because my SSCE results were out. I had passed beyond my expectations so I was very happy to tell Uncle and Aunty my result. Uncle came in early from work that day.

Me: Uncle, welcome back.

Uncle Johnny: Ah! Gloria, how are you?

Me: I'm fine, Uncle, my results came out today and I passed very well.

Uncle Johnny: Wow, wonderful! Let me see it.

He glanced over it.

Uncle Johnny: We should celebrate it. Go and get ready.

I wore my best clothes and that evening Uncle

Johnny took me around to eat at a good restaurant. I really enjoyed myself that day. We got home later than usual and I got ready for bed.

In the middle of the night, I was awakened by a stranger in my bed. The person covered my mouth and tried to tear off my nightgown. I tried to scream but I could not. I eventually struggled and was finally able to switch on the light and Uncle Johnny was above me.

Me: Uncle, what are you doing?

Uncle Johnny: Just shut up and lay down.

I tried to struggle but Uncle Johnny used his strength to overpower me so I could barely move. Then I felt a sharp pain. Every movement only made it worse so I laid there crying and screaming for Uncle Johnny to stop but he did not. Eventually, he got up and left the room. I quickly got up and locked my room door. There was blood all over my sheets. Embarrassed, I took the sheets off, scrubbed the stain from the bed, washed my gown and bed sheets that night, and then cleaned myself up before going back to bed.

The following day, Aunty Dayo got back. I was still too scared to come outside. She eventually knocked on my door and I came out to greet her. Uncle Johnny was behind her smiling. Uncle Johnny told her I had not been feeling too well so Aunty Dayo told me to go back to sleep.

The month following was awkward. I avoided Uncle Johnny as much as I could. I locked my room all the time and stayed indoors.

Part Three - Life is a Hustle

Aunty Dayo and I had gone shopping for some of the items when I felt nauseous and vomited all over the floor. Aunty Dayo looked at me strange and said we had to go to the hospital. On arriving at the hospital, the doctor informed her I had to take a pregnancy test. When the test results came out, Aunty Dayo told me I was pregnant. Once we got back home, Aunty Dayo started yelling and beating me.

Aunty Dayo: Look at you, after all we have done. Who did you get pregnant for?

At that point, I was crying.

Me: Aunty, I did not do anything. I swear to God. I have been following everything that you told me to do. I don't have a boyfriend.

Aunty Dayo: So how did you get pregnant? Ehn? Abi is the doctor lying?

Me (crying): Aunty, I don't know.

Uncle Johnny walked in.

Uncle Johnny: What is going on? I could hear the noise from outside.

Aunty Dayo: Please, ask her oh. The doctor said she is pregnant.

Uncle Johnny: What? Gloria! Is that true?

Me (pointing at Uncle Johnny): Aunty, he did it. When you traveled for training, he raped me.

Aunty Dayo slapped me and I raised my hand to my cheek, staring back at her in surprise

Aunty Dayo: So now you are lying against your uncle?

Me (my face was throbbing): No, Aunty, why will I lie? He raped me. He did.

Aunty Dayo stares at Uncle Johnny in disbelief.

Uncle Johnny: That girl is a liar, why will I rape my own niece? God forbid. Gloria, you must be out of your mind.

Aunty Dayo looks back at me.

Aunty Dayo: I give you until tomorrow morning, you better tell me the truth or else, you will leave my house, you hear? You cannot bear any bastard in my house.

The following morning came around. I did not have any words to say. Aunty Dayo did not believe me. Uncle Johnny had convinced her that I was lying. I was sent packing and left their home with no place to go.

That night I slept in the balcony of a shop. The following day, I wandered around looking for food and help. A lady that owned a restaurant felt pity on me and hired me to work in her restaurant. I was paid good enough to care for myself and the unborn baby. The restaurant owner also let me sleep in her boys-quarters.

Part Four - My Bundle of Joy

My bundle of joy arrived on my 17th birthday. He was a blessing from God. Restaurant madam was so happy. She showed me how to breastfeed him, bathe him, and she bought a few items for the both of us. I named my bundle of joy after my father. I called him Akpan.

177

Akpan was a bright child. He had a personality that cheered everyone and as I watched him grow, everyone complimented me on what a happy baby he was.

As Akpan grew up, he was top of his class in mathematics and won a Federal Government scholarship that afforded him the opportunity to go to a great public school. Akpan loved to play football. He was so good at it that his nickname was 'JayJay' for the soccer player Jay-Jay Okocha. People used to say he would grow up to play for Nigeria and win the World Cup for us.

Unfortunately, two incidents happened at the same time that changed our lives. The restaurant owner lost her restaurant to an unknown fire source so she could not support us financially anymore. Also, a new regime of government took over that did not continue supporting the scholarship so Akpan was forced to stop schooling at the age of 10 years old. I could not continue to pay his school fees.

To survive, we bought some few items with the little money I had saved and started hawking those food items on the highway. It was not an easy job. We had to run with the car to get the passengers to buy our product and then chase the car again to get the money and give them change. Life was very tough, we now survived on bread in the morning, pure water and biscuit in the afternoon, and garri at night. As tough as it was, Akpan maintained his charisma.

Part Five - Save Akpan

One morning, Akpan woke up with a running nose and cough. His eyes looked a little bit red so I thought he just needed some more rest and I allowed him to stay home and get some sleep. When I got back home, Akpan had some spots and blisters on his skin. I became scared and called the restaurant madam to look at him. She recommended a traditional herbalist to look at him since we did not have money to take him to the hospital.

The herbalist visited every morning for a week to rub a smelly medicine on Akpan's body but he was not getting any better. Each day, Akpan got worse and I was becoming more concerned. By the end of the week, Akpan's body was completely covered in tiny spots. I ran to restaurant madam

Me: Madam, Akpan is not getting any better oh. I am getting really worried, he cannot even play around anymore.

Madam: I was thinking of coming to check on you. We have to take that boy to the hospital. I know you don't have money but let us get there and see first.

I bathed Akpan to try to get off the herbalist medicine smell from his body and we took him in Madam's car to the nearest hospital. As we got to the hospital, Madam looked for a place to park while I rushed in to find any help. There was a lady wearing a nursing uniform at the entrance.

Me: Good morning ma, abeg please, my son is sick. I need to see a doctor.

Reception Nurse: Where is your son?

Me: He is outside, my madam is bringing him in. Is the doctor around?

Reception Nurse: Yes he is but you have to pay the 20,000 naira deposit first

Restaurant Madam carried in Akpan.

Me: Nurse, I take God beg you. This is my son, please let us see the doctor, I have 8000 naira here and I promise I will bring the balance in tomorrow.

Reception Nurse: Sorry madam, we cannot do credit. I have been instructed to collect the balance before the doctor can see them. If I disobey that rule, I will lose my job so abeg madam, go and find the 20,000 naira.

Restaurant Madam pulled me to the side and to my surprise, she gave me the 20,000 naira to pay for Akpan.

I thanked madam profusely and paid for the hospital. The reception nurse upon collecting the funds called the other nurses to take him in. A couple of hours later, I was called in to see the doctor and was informed that my son had chicken pox. It would take a week or more to completely heal him. The treatment would cost 80,000 naira and I had to make 50% deposit to commence treatment on him.

I went out of the doctor's office and told restaurant madam. She took me home to get the last of my savings, it was 5,000 naira. She added another 2,000 naira. I went back to the hospital to deposit the 7,000 naira but the hospital would not commence treatment on him until I brought back the remaining deposit balance. I was devastated. My boy was dying in there and I did not have any means to help him. I ran outside. There were fancy luxury cars driving past me. I thought these people could help me. I started moving towards their car and asking for help but they had their windows rolled up and did not look my way. I walked up and down the streets to beg for money, any amount. I was only able to raise 500 naira.

I went back to the hospital and begged to have my son treated but the hospital would not budge. They discharged my son, sick as he was. The doctor recommended some drugs to help. I bought those drugs and took my son home. Akpan took the medicine and laid down quietly. The following morning, when I woke up, Akpan was not breathing. I shook him, poured water over his head but my baby would not move.

Akpan was dead.

I screamed. The neighbors gathered around.

Restaurant madam was speechless and crying. She held me close. Everyone was sympathetic. They gave their condolences and left. I could not hear them. All I could see was Akpan's body in front of me, covered, not moving, not smiling at me, not hugging me.

Part Six - A Friend

It took me over a year to get myself together after Akpan's death. I started selling again, I started smiling again but on many days, I would find myself sleepless at night, crying over my lost boy.

Restaurant madam had helped me to find a job in another restaurant and I started working there. The job was doing good and helped me to get back to myself. In all these years, I never went back to Uncle Johnny's house. I heard he and Aunty Dayo separated because they could not have a child together.

One day at the restaurant, I got a call to serve the new customers that just came in; a bunch of men that looked like they had a lot of money to spend so I put on my best behavior to welcome them.

Me: Hello sirs, what can I offer you today?

They each gave their orders and I left to go place the order to the cook in the back. I was standing there when the restaurant owner came to me and informed me that one of the customers had another order for me. So I stepped out again smiling and went to their table. The customer requesting an additional order was a man named Ben.

Customer (extending his hand): Hi, my name is Ben.

I noticed he had a funny accent. I squatted a little to greet him as a sign of respect for customers.

Ben: Are you going to leave my hand hanging?

I looked over to the back room and the madam

was over there nodding me to accept his hand shake so I shook him.

Me: My name is Gloria. What is your order, sir?

Ben: Yeah, your madam told me your name. So do you work here daily?

This was becoming annoying.

Me: Yes, I do. Please, can I have your order?

Ben: Oh sorry, I would like to be your friend, Gloria.

Me: Thanks but no. Is there anything else I can help you with?

Ben: No, that was it.

Me: Ok, please let me know if you need anything else.

I walked away to the back. I could hear his friends laughing at him but that was not my problem. I served them their order and I noticed Ben kept staring at me each time I walked out. It was quite uncomfortable. After the end of the meal, they left a huge tip and I was grateful that I got their table.

The following day, it was my turn to work in the back to do the dishes, but then, madam called me. There was a particular customer that wanted me to serve his table. I cleaned up and walked outside and Ben was sitting there. This time he was by himself.

Ben: Hi, there.

Me: What would you like, sir?

Ben: Just 5 minutes of your time, please.

Me: I am working.

Ben: I know I already talked to your madam and she said you can take 5 minutes off.

I looked over to my madam and she was nodding with approval.

Me: So, you won't bother me after this?

Ben: It depends, if you don't want me to, I won't.

We walked to the street and Ben started talking.

Ben: I'm sorry that I showed up to your workplace. I just wanted a few minutes of your time to talk to you. I saw you yesterday and after our brief discussion, I was convinced that I would not talk to you again but I could not get you off my mind. Please, I just want to be your friend that is all. I don't want anything else from you.

Me: What does that mean? Being friends with me?

Ben (smiling): It means being there for you when you need me to be, that is all.

I said ok and Ben walked me back to the restaurant. This was the first time anyone had asked to be my friend. It was a bit strange but I was welcome to it. We got back to the restaurant and I shook his hand. As I walked in, I heard him call the restaurant owner "Aunty". I found out later that it was not out of respect. The restaurant owner told me Ben was her nephew and was visiting Nigeria from the United States for a little bit. She thought I could use a friend so she told him about me and Akpan. He was very interested in meeting me and told her he wanted to be friends with me.

Ben and I became friends. I had no trust for men so we met in public places and spent a good amount of time talking and getting to know each other. Ben was very kind; he never pushed me to talk about anything that I was uncomfortable talking about. I told him about my parents, Uncle Johnny, Aunty Dayo and Akpan. He told me about himself as well. His dad had passed away when he was 20 and had to take responsibility of his family at a young age. He decided to go to United States to study business management and ended up staying there to get work experience. His plans were to come back to Nigeria in a few years and grow his father's business.

Ben left for the United States but kept in touch. He would call his Aunty and ask to speak to me. One day, his Aunty gave me a phone. She said Ben sent it to her for me. I was excited. I had never owned a phone in my life. Ben called me daily to make sure I was fine. He would send me money and gifts and call just to make sure I got them. He encouraged me to return back to school to start my education. I took the JAMB exam again and got accepted to the university.

A year later, Ben returned to Nigeria and began work at his father's company. He hired me to work in the company part-time as I was still continuing my studies. Upon graduation, he offered me a full time job.

About the Author

Titi Sule was born in Port Harcourt, Nigeria. She enjoys writing to inspire people. This collection was written to discuss adversities in many societies. These individuals have lived through hardships such as domestic violence, child abuse, unemployment, marriage pressure, etc. that sometimes are kept silent even though the pain and trauma still exists. This book was written to inspire us all to live our best life no matter life hardships. What is within us is stronger than what is in our way.

UnSpoken Voices

Stories by

Titi Sule

Question and Topics for Discussion

1. Most of the stories in *UnSpoken Voices* are from females. With progress made in society, do you believe women are now treated fairly in your society? In what ways are you seeing unequal treatment of women? How can we change this?

2. In *Chances Are*, did you find yourself forgiving Emeka for stealing from the rich given his unemployment situation? Do you think that Funmi should forgive him? Why?

3. In *Flee*, was Bisi to eager to marry that she overlooked Bola's violent behavior? Do you think a woman should call off her engagement given a first-hand experience of her fiancé violent behavior? Do you think a woman should stay in her marriage after her husband has been violent and sought forgiveness and therapy?

4. In *The Park Tree*, if you were in Emeka's shoes and found the body, would you have reported the case to the police? Can you relate to a similar horror story in the hands of the law?

5. In Ejiro's story, *Love Lost*, we covered the case of a mother who left her child. In some places, mothers do not have custody rights due to tradition. If you were in Ejiro's mother's shoes what would you do?

6. In *Victim of Society*, who would you consider to be the victim and why? Kunle, Sade, or Sade's son Femi? Why are some societies obsessed about marriage?

7. Anyone should have the right to be educated. Is this still a problem in your society? Why are some women not allowed to be educated? Do you believe education of the female child should be left to the government as law or to

the parent of the female child?

8. In Boarding schools, some people would argue that the harsh experience toughens children. Do you agree? Did you have a pleasant boarding experience? Do you know someone who did not?

9. Save Him Save Me details really tough adversity through rape and death. How can someone like Gloria learn to trust again?

10. Have you been dealt with adversity that you have overcome?

Made in the USA
Columbia, SC
09 June 2020

10453875R00119